"Ria," Taylor whispered, "there's snow sparkling on your hair."

She shook her head. He watched the sensuous movement of her loose hair. "It's beautiful. Black as midnight. Shiny and silky. So seductive." What was seductive was the way he threaded his fingers through it and spread it over the soft silver fox of her coat, his eyes moving over her face, then down her pale throat.

Ria shivered. "It'll be warm in here soon."

"Baby, it's already warm."

Stepping closer, he cupped her face between his hands and stroked her cold cheeks with his thumbs, warming them instantly. He brushed his lips against hers, at first light and questing, then firm and insistent. Ria gasped and turned her head away.

"I'm sorry . . . I had no right. But I just had to kiss you."

She lifted her face to his again. Her eyes were greedy for the sight of him wanting her, needing her.

"In that case—" He kissed her then, and this time a current of desire sizzled between them, threatening to engulf them both. . . .

WHAT ARE *LOVESWEPT* ROMANCES?

They are stories of true romance and touching emotion. We believe those two very important ingredients are constants in our highly sensual and very believable stories in the *LOVESWEPT* line. Our goal is to give you, the reader, stories of consistently high quality that may sometimes make you laugh, sometimes make you cry, but are always fresh and creative and contain many delightful surprises within their pages.

Most romance fans read an enormous number of books. Those they truly love, they keep. Others may be traded with friends and soon forgotten. We hope that each *LOVESWEPT* romance will be a treasure—a ''keeper.'' We will always try to publish

LOVE STORIES YOU'LL NEVER FORGET
BY AUTHORS YOU'LL ALWAYS REMEMBER

The Editors

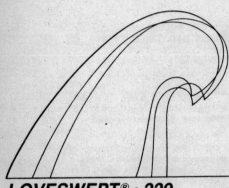

LOVESWEPT® • 229

Sandra Brown
Tidings of Great Joy

BANTAM BOOKS
TORONTO · NEW YORK · LONDON · SYDNEY · AUCKLAND

TIDINGS OF GREAT JOY

A Bantam Book / January 1988

ISBN 0-553-21850-6

Published simultaneously in the United States and Canada

*Bantam Books are published by Bantam Books, Inc. Its trade-
mark, consisting of the words "Bantam Books" and the por-
trayal of a rooster, is Registered in U.S. Patent and Trademark
Office and in other countries. Marca Registrada. Bantam
Books, Inc., 666 Fifth Avenue, New York, New York 10103.*

PRINTED IN THE UNITED STATES OF AMERICA

O   0 9 8 7 6 5 4 3 2 1

Prologue

"I'm pregnant."

Taylor MacKensie's eyes skidded to a stop about halfway up Ria Lavender's shinbone, bringing to a halt his prurient appraisal of her shapely legs. His gaze swung up to her face. She didn't appear to have lost her faculties, but it was either that or he hadn't heard her correctly. "I'm sorry?"

"I'm pregnant."

Taylor lowered himself into the leather chair behind his desk and tried his damnedest to work up enough spit to swallow. "Congratulations" didn't seem a proper response. She'd hurled the two words at him like darts. The statement was more than a description of her physical condition. It issued a challenge. That challenge was echoed in her dark green eyes.

"Thanks for telling me, but I could have waited for a birth announcement," he said flippantly.

"You're the first to know."

"Any particular reason why?"

"A very good reason."

"Are you implying that I have something to do with your pregnancy?"

"No, I'm not *implying* anything. The baby is yours."

Cool as a cucumber was Ria Lavender, but Taylor went hot all over. And he could forget swallowing any time soon. His salivary glands were dammed up, and he doubted they would ever resume operation. To hide his astonishment he laughed shortly. "Is this a joke?"

"Hardly, Mr. MacKensie. Farce has never been my favorite form of comedy."

"Nor mine. But that sure as hell is what this sounds like," he said testily.

"Take my word for it that no one is going to come barging in here and poke a shotgun in your back."

"I wouldn't be surprised by anything after this. Just where do you get off, waltzing in here and dropping this bombshell?"

"I didn't waltz," Ria replied evenly. "I made an appointment, went through all the necessary and proper channels to talk to a city councilman, and—"

"Ms. Lavender, excuse me, but when a citizen of this city makes an appointment with me, I expect we'll discuss upcoming bond elections or tax laws or extended bus service."

"Maybe I should have called on you in your company office. But I was afraid you'd think I wanted to see you on business."

He ran his fingers through his thick, dark mahogany hair. "I can't believe you're serious."

"I am."

"This isn't a trick? A practical joke?"

"I do not play practical jokes," she said with an air of superiority.

"Well, how the hell should I know that? I barely know you."

They stared at each other across the polished surface of his desk. Ria was the first to look away. Taylor detected the color rising in her cheeks. About time, he thought. He'd felt flushed and hot ever since she'd come in.

It should have made her blush to acknowledge just how well he *did* know her. Especially since they'd only met once before.

One

"Oh, excuse me!"

"No apology necessary."

"Didn't I stick your finger with my toothpick?"

"A few stitches and it'll be as good as new." He shrugged negligently and sucked on his injured finger.

Ria laughed. "I'm sorry."

"Forget it."

"Please take the shrimp."

"Uh-uh. If you've had your eye on that particular shrimp, I wouldn't dream of depriving you of it."

Ria smiled up into an incredibly handsome face. It sat atop one heck of a good body, too. Tall, slender, outfitted in a dark three-piece suit, white shirt, red tie. *Red* tie? Well, it was Christmas Eve. The tie and matching silk handkerchief, three corners of which were peeking out of his breast pocket, were his concessions to the holiday. Where other men might look silly because of such frivolity, this one had the panache to carry it off well without its threatening his masculinity. The wide white smile helped. Guileless, open, warm. Growing warmer by the second. Or was that the furnace in her own belly being stoked by that smile and his dazzling blue eyes?

"Ria Lavender." She switched her plate from right hand to left so she could shake hands with him.

"Taylor MacKensie." He didn't have a plate yet, only the cocktail toothpick that had been about to skewer the same shrimp her toothpick had aimed for. He shook hands with her.

"*The* Taylor MacKensie?" she asked. Her hand wanted to snuggle in the warm, firm clasp of his forever.

"Is there a *the* Taylor MacKensie?"

His eyes crinkled at the corners when he smiled. He liked the outdoors. And the outdoors liked him. Its ravages had saved him from being pretty. Although that square jaw was far from what one could define as pretty. "Are you the famous City Councilman MacKensie, candidate for mayor?"

He bowed stiffly. "The same. It's a pleasure, Mrs. Lavender."

Ria cocked her head to one side. "Very clever."

"What?"

"*Mrs.* Lavender. You're clearly manipulating me into telling you whether or not I'm married."

He lowered his voice to a confidential pitch. "The suspense is killing me."

"It's Ms. and has never been Mrs."

"Hot damn," he said, snapping his fingers. "I've always had phenomenal good luck."

Immensely pleased with what they saw, they stared at each other until someone jostled Taylor from behind. "Uh, more shrimp?" he asked courteously.

"I've already got an immodest number, but thank you."

He glanced down the length of the holiday buffet table, shopping the variety of food. "Can we talk turkey?"

Ria liked his sense of humor. So far there was nothing about him she didn't like. And she loved turkey. She flashed him her own rendition of a dazzling smile. "Please."

He picked up a plate for himself and they moved along the buffet, serving themselves, though food was now the last thing on their minds. The Grahams' Christmas Eve open house had taken on new interest. Each had attended the party out of a sense of obligation and had planned to leave after making an appearance. Taylor forgot the excuse he had intended to give the hosts for having to leave early. Ria was relieved of having to dream up one.

"Where shall we sit?" Taylor scanned the crowded living room, looking for two empty seats close together. There were single chairs scattered here and there, but he seemed disinclined to claim one, and Ria was glad.

Spontaneously she asked him, "How friendly do you feel like being?"

"I can be downright rude and still sleep nights," he told her with a devilish grin.

"Then follow me."

Winking conspiratorially at the bartender, Taylor picked up a bottle of chilled champagne and two glasses. Ria headed for the staircase. A Persian runner was secured to the steps with brass rods, but the staircase still appeared to be contemporary because of its cantilevered construction.

"That is a really knockout dress," Taylor remarked as they climbed the stairs.

She glanced at him over her shoulder. His eyes were trained on her spine, which was left bare by the low back of her thickly sequined blue dress. It

was cut equally low in the front, dipping to a deep
V between her breasts. The skirt was narrow and
was hemmed straight across her knees. The waist
was cinched with a wide self-belt. The padded
shoulders were decorated with a design formed of
silver sequins. A matching sequin-covered clasp
held back one side of her long, straight hair.

"Thank you."

"You're welcome."

The stairs led to a gallery, which overlooked the
rooms below. "This was a great idea," Taylor said
as they glanced down at the noisy crowd.

"I'm glad I thought of it too."

They stood at the railing for a moment, staring
at each other. He looked much hungrier for a bite
of her lower lip than he did for any of the food on
his plate. She would have enjoyed being nibbled.
"This way," she said gruffly.

She led him into a spacious room lit only by the
fire in the fireplace and the mammoth Christmas
tree in the corner. The room was furnished with
white leather sofas and chairs as soft and plush as
marshmallows. The pile of the butterscotch-colored
carpet almost swallowed the high heels on Ria's
black satin shoes. She crossed the room and set
her plate on the glass-topped coffee table.

"The light switch is on your left," she told Taylor. He was standing in the wide doorway, appre-
ciatively surveying the room. "But if your hands
are full I can get it."

"Do you mind if we leave it like this?"

Holding his gaze, she shook her head. "Actually, I prefer it this way."

"Me too."

He joined her where she stood, between the sofa
and the fireplace, and by tacit agreement they sat
on the floor. Ria folded her legs beneath her hips.

Taylor sat with one knee raised, his back against the couch.

Expertly, he opened the champagne so that it only burped loudly, but didn't spew. Ria tipped her head to salute this expertise and held up her glass. He poured. When his glass was brimming, he raised it to hers.

"Merry Christmas, Ria."

"Merry Christmas, Taylor."

Looking at each other over their glasses, they drank. He smacked his lips. "Far better than the champagne punch."

"Hm." She let the champagne bubble and sparkle inside her mouth before swallowing its icy heat. "There's nothing like the real thing."

Taylor popped an olive-crowned canapé into his mouth. "How did you know where to find this getaway room?"

"I designed it."

Obviously impressed, his eyebrows climbed up his forehead a fraction. "Interior design?"

"No. I only made recommendations on how it should be decorated. I designed it from the studs out. I was the architect."

"You were the architect who designed this house?"

She nodded. Methodically chewing a cherry tomato stuffed with crab salad, Taylor surveyed the room again, looking at it from a new perspective. From the carpet beneath them to the cathedral ceiling, he liked what he saw. Ria could tell that by the way his eyes lingered on every structural detail.

She was expecting a compliment, so when he said, "It's snowing," she was surprised. She tilted her head back and saw that flakes as big and fluffy as goose down were settling on the clear skylights overhead.

"How lovely, a white Christmas," she said with hushed reverence.

"I'm moved to break out in song. Want me to?"

"Can you sing?"

"I sound great in the shower."

"Then maybe you'd better not."

"You don't believe I can sing? Guess you'll just have to join me in the shower to find out."

Ria calmly took a sip of champagne. The innuendo wasn't offensive. His smile was too disarming. Still, it was sexy, just as he had intended it to be.

Setting her glass down, she glanced up at him through her lashes. "You're as dangerous as they say, Mr. MacKensie."

"Who say?" He was suspiciously sniffing at an anchovy.

"Everybody who's ever accused you of being a lady-killer."

"Oh, them." He shrugged dismissively, both at the allegation and the anchovy, which he returned to his plate. "Political enemies started those rumors."

"Or women scorned."

"I suppose there are a few of those." His smile was rueful.

"I didn't mean to imply that you're not a serious politician and businessman," she said sincerely. From reading newspaper articles about him, she knew that he owned and operated an electrical-contracting business. "Despite all the mud your opponent is slinging, I think you'll win the mayor's race."

"Will you vote for me?"

"If you'll pour me another glass of champagne." Coquettishly, she held up her glass.

He topped it off, then refilled his own as he

said, "I wish all votes were as easy to come by. Why are you going to vote for me?"

"Because you're a progressive thinker. Maybe a tad too outspoken and aggressive."

"Bleeker called me 'street tough.' "

She laughed over the label his opponent had stuck on him. "The description fits, though I'm sure Bleeker didn't mean it as a compliment. I don't think you'd ever let anybody bully you."

"You're right. I grew up in the suburbs, an all-American kid. But I held my own with the bad guys."

"You impress me as a mover and shaker. Some people are afraid of change, but for a long time I've thought that this city needed some changes."

"I only hope I'll be able to move and shake all the deadwood on the city council. If I'm elected," he grumbled. Then seconds later in the same tone of voice he said, "Damn."

"What?"

"I forgot to get turkey after all."

"Here, have some." She offered him her plate.

He held up both hands. "No, really, I couldn't."

Was she getting tipsy, or was his protest actually that overstated and funny? "Go on. I insist. After all, I took the shrimp away from you." She picked up a sliver of white meat and extended it to him.

He stared at it as though it were the last morsel of food on earth but he was unworthy of eating it. "You won the shrimp in a fair fight."

"Please?" She lifted her hand closer to his mouth.

"Well, if you insist."

He bit into the succulent slice of turkey breast. It had never occurred to Ria that teeth could be sexy, but she felt that bite right above her belly button. It was a thrilling sensation. His breath was warm against her fingers. The turkey was so tender, it could have been cut with a fork, but he moved his head from side to side slightly, as though tearing at it. The bottom of her stomach dropped away, as if she'd just cannoned over the highest peak of the roller coaster.

He said, "Delicious."

"Nice and juicy."

"Uh-huh."

She realized that he was looking at her mouth. His eyes were as unblinking as a predatory cat's. She felt vulnerable beneath that steady blue gaze. Her hand trembled slightly as she reached for the stem of her glass of champagne.

Only when she moved and broke the spell did he stop staring. "I like this Christmas tree better than the one downstairs," he said.

Ria was glad he had changed the subject. It relieved the tension in her chest. The party noise coming from downstairs was a faraway roar. Occasionally a burst of laughter would puncture the quiet, but basically the only sound in the room was that of the popping applewood logs in the grate and the sexy whisper of evening clothes each time one of them moved. A take-your-shoes-off-and-be-comfortable kind of mood had settled over them. She had never felt so relaxed. Anywhere. At any time. Nor had she ever felt so breathless with anticipation. As a safety precaution, she kept her shoes on.

She looked at the Christmas tree. Its fragrant green branches were decorated with twinkling colored lights, glass balls, tinsel, and candy canes. "I like this one best too," she said. "I prefer the old-fashioned kind."

"They don't count unless you can smell them."

"Right. The one downstairs in the living room is gorgeous, but so formal."

"Untouchable."

"It was done by a professional decorator. You can tell that the family decorated this one. The ornaments are irregularly spaced."

Her host and hostess, the Grahams, had several grown children and numerous grandchildren. Ria could imagine the laughter, the affectionate bantering, the squeals of pleasure that would echo off these walls when the myriad gift-wrapped boxes were ripped open the following morning.

Leaning closer to her, Taylor whispered, "I'll bet if you looked close, you'd see some of those ornaments are tarnished and broken."

She nodded dreamily. "But they're the most cherished ones. The older the better. They're the reminders of past Christmases, and will never be thrown out."

He touched her cheek with the backs of his fingers. "The lady architect has a sentimental streak."

Pleasurably, she broke out in goose bumps. "I confess."

No longer pretending to eat, they abandoned their plates. Another kind of hunger had set in. There was no sense in denying it. Unabashedly Taylor stared at her. "I've never had a battle of toothpicks with someone as pretty as you. Are you sure you're real?"

It was on the tip of Ria's tongue to say, "Touch me and see," but she thought better of it. He looked ready to pounce and gobble. If the rumors were true, Taylor MacKensie needed no encouragement. Whether such rumors were maliciously sowed by his political enemies or not, they must have some basis in truth. Ria was too level-headed to be swayed by a smooth line and a seductive smile. But she was having too good a time to rebuff him. So she decided to keep them on a friendly and flirting basis.

"Oh, I'm real, all right. What you didn't know," Ria drawled, "was that my stomach was growling most indelicately when I spotted that fat pink shrimp."

"Hush, now." He laid his index finger vertically against her lips. "You're making my mouth water."

Time out! Ria thought. So much for flirting. It was no longer harmless. Taylor MacKensie was making *her* mouth water. The softly lit room, the fireplace, the Christmas ambience, were having a dangerous effect on her. She felt herself losing control of the situation and knew she had to get it back.

"Maybe we'd better go downstairs and mingle."

He frowned, but seemed to recognize the advisability of that. This was getting way out of hand way too fast. "I guess we'd better. There are lots of voters down there."

He stood up and offered her his hand, which she gladly accepted. She should have eaten more. The champagne had gone straight to her head. And to her thighs. They were rubbery. She swayed slightly as she stood up. He slipped an arm around her waist to steady her, pressing her against him briefly.

"Okay?" His voice was merely a low growl that reminded her of animal mating sounds.

"Yes, fine."

He released her, but she felt his reluctance to do so. Carrying their plates with them, they descended the staircase. "I like the house," he said. "Very innovative. Contemporary without being stark."

"I was pleased with how it turned out," Ria replied modestly.

"Don't let her get by with that."

They turned at the sound of their hostess's voice. Decked out in plaid taffeta that whistled as she approached them, Mrs. Graham beamed a smile upon Ria and embraced her affectionately. "She's far too modest, Taylor. I'm glad you've met our town's most ingenious, original architect. I threw this bash solely for the purpose of showing off Ria's masterpiece."

"I think you have excellent taste," Taylor said, smiling his charming smile. "Both in houses and in architects."

Mrs. Graham took Ria's arm and drew her away from Taylor's side. "A friend of mine has been dying to meet you, Ria. She's pea green over my house and wants one of her own. She owns a lovely piece of property— For heaven's sake, Taylor, don't look so downcast. You'll catch up with Ria later. Now, be a good boy and spread yourself around. I think some of the men are playing pool in the game room."

He caught up with Ria three-quarters of an hour later. She was one of a group collected around the white grand piano. Taylor overcame the decked halls, boughs of holly, not to mention the fa-la-la-la-la-la-la-la-las, in order to reach her side and join her on the chorus of an ancient Yuletide carol.

"Hi."

"Hi. Did you play pool?"

"Yep. And won. I didn't collect my bets, though. I'm always charitable at Christmastime."

Another song was already underway. They joined in. In the middle of the second verse, Ria leaned back. "You were right. You—"

"What? I can't hear you." He leaned down far enough for her lips to graze the peach fuzz on his earlobe.

"You were right," she repeated. He tilted his head and looked down at her quizzically. "You can't sing."

Laughing, he squeezed her elbow.

The party began to wind down. The weather was rapidly becoming a factor in people's getting home safely. Together, Ria and Taylor drifted toward the room where a maid was holding coats. When she came back with Ria's, Ria saw Taylor give a start of surprise. He took the full-length silver fox from the maid and draped it over Ria's shoulders, slinging his overcoat over his arm. They progressed to the front door, where the Grahams were bidding everyone good night.

"It was lovely. Thank you for inviting me," Ria said to the distinguished couple. She kissed her hostess on the cheek.

Mrs. Graham patted Ria's hand. "The party was lovely because my house is lovely, and my house is lovely because you are lovely. And if you think I'm going to let you drive off this hill alone in weather like this, you've got another think coming."

"I'm used to driving in snow," Ria exclaimed.

"But not down that sheer cliff we mistakenly call a road," Mr. Graham said.

"I'll be happy to drive her home." Taylor stepped forward with the bravura of an Alamo volunteer crossing the sword-drawn line in the sand.

"Excellent," Mrs. Graham said with a wide smile. "Darling, be sure to contribute to Taylor's campaign fund," she told her husband.

"But my car," Ria protested. She wasn't accustomed to being looked after like a child.

"I'll get someone to drive it down to you tomorrow. You'd better go now, before that icy hill gets worse. Good night, dears, and Merry Christmas."

The Grahams waved them off perfunctorily and turned their attention to other departing guests. Without causing a scene, Ria had no choice but to submit to the nudge Taylor gave her elbow.

"You don't really mind, do you?" he asked her, bending his head against the blowing snow.

"No. Do you?"

"Of course not."

"They put you on the spot. You didn't have much choice."

"Sure, I did. I told you earlier that I can be downright rude." His grip on her arm tightened. "Besides, even if they hadn't asked, I would have offered you a lift. I wouldn't like it either if you tried to drive home alone in this weather."

"I'm sure I can handle a little snow."

He glanced up at the sky. "It's more like a blizzard. And remember," he said, squeezing her elbow, "I know how much champagne you guzzled."

Laughing together, they moved along the row of parked cars in the driveway until they reached a new Corvette. As he fumbled in his pocket for the keys, he said, "You know, I'm still not sure you're real. You're gorgeous, talented, smart, amusing. You've got your own jewelry and—"

"These?" she asked, indicating the chandeliers of rhinestones dangling from her ears. "These are costume."

"But this isn't." He ran his fingers through the fur collar of her coat. For warmth, she had bunched it up close to her ears. The coat had been her one material indulgence when she joined the most prestigious firm of architects in the city. She had chosen to wrap herself in yards of silver fox rather than the leather interior of a fancy automobile.

"You've already got your own fur coat, on top of all your other attributes. There's got to be something wrong with you." He peered at her through the falling snow. "You must have rotten teeth."

She swatted at his nose before ducking into the car. The road was much more perilous than Ria would have felt comfortable driving down. She was glad the Grahams had insisted that she ride with someone, although she wasn't certain that Taylor MacKensie was the wisest choice.

She felt muzzy. Her ears were ringing, and it wasn't the echo of Christmas Eve church bells. She wasn't sure all her toes were still there. That could be due to walking through the snow in evening pumps. But how could she account for feeling so warm everywhere else? The car's heater was blasting them with hot air, true, but the heat she felt was generated from beneath her own skin.

Philosophically she determined that she had imbibed too much Christmas cheer or Taylor MacKensie's masculine magnetism had made her high. Either way, she was ashamed of herself for behaving so foolishly.

The windshield wipers were clanking as hypnotically as a metronome. Snowflakes merrily danced in the beam of the headlights. The night had a surreal quality. But if this was fantasy, who needed reality? While it lasted, why not enjoy it?

"Music?"

"Pardon?" He nodded toward the radio. "Yes, please." She winked at him. "If you promise not to sing along."

"Looks like they're all playing Christmas carols tonight," he said after punching in several stations.

"That's fine with me. I enjoy hearing them once a year."

"Yeah, me too. How come you're spending Christmas Eve alone?" he asked suddenly. "I'd have thought there'd be a dozen beaux lined up at your door begging for a date on the night before Christmas."

Ria thanked him for the compliment. "The man I'm seeing is away."

"There's a man?"

"Yes. He has an elderly mother in Florida. He's spending the holiday with her."

Taylor digested that information without comment. "Parents?"

"They decided to take a trip to England to visit friends. They were reluctant to go at this time of year, but I urged them to. After all, Christmas Eve is just like any other night."

"Do you really believe that?" he asked, looking across at her.

For as long as it was safe, their eyes held. "No," she said softly, shaking her head, "but I didn't want my folks to miss this trip on my account."

"What about the man?"

"I couldn't be responsible for his neglecting his mother." To divert the conversation away from herself, she asked, "What about you? Why are you alone? No family?"

"My dad, but he has another family now. He and Janey live in Los Angeles." He explained that his father had remarried a considerably younger woman after his mother's death. They'd had two children together. "I've got a stepbrother and stepsister young enough to be my own kids. I'm always welcome at their house, but I think my being there makes everybody uncomfortable, afraid of doing or saying the wrong thing."

"Friends?" She meant, specifically, girlfriends, and hated herself for wanting to know.

"I was invited to go on a ski trip with a group of people."

"How large a group?"

He grinned, letting her know that he knew what she was fishing for. "Seven. Among them the woman I'm seeing. I backed out at the last minute."

"Why? Did you have a tiff?"

"No. The day before yesterday I sprained my ankle playing racquet ball, and decided it would be really stupid to ski on it. That's when we had the tiff."

"She went without you?"

He shrugged. "She's a very independent lady."

"Funny, how Christmas can either be hectic and exuberant, or empty and sad."

"It depends on whether it's shared with someone or spent alone."

"I guess. Although it could be terrible if shared with someone you didn't love, or even like. I think that would be worse than spending it alone."

Ria had given him her street address when they left the Grahams. He drove straight to it without asking for directions. The young, volatile candidate for mayor knew his city well.

Pulling to a stop at the curb in front of her house, he turned the key and cut the Corvette's motor. The windshield wipers ceased their rhythmic clacking. "O Come All Ye Faithful" fell silent in mid-verse. Neither passenger in the car moved. Finally, at the same time, they turned to each other and started talking.

"Thank—"

"I could be—"

"I'm sorry."

"I'm sorry. Ladies first."

"I was just saying thank you for the ride."

Taylor turned his head and stared through the windshield, which was quickly becoming blanketed with snow. Ria could see him gnawing the inside of his jaw. He swiveled his head back around quickly. "I could be talked into a cup of coffee."

She hesitated only a few heartbeats before nodding. He got out and came around to open her door. His fingers curled firmly around her upper arm as they made their way up the treacherously icy sidewalk.

Ria took her key from her silver metal evening

bag and opened the front door. The warm air inside embraced them like an old and beloved friend. Ria flipped on a wall switch. The end-table lamp didn't come on, as she had expected it to. Instead her Christmas tree lit up.

"Oh, I forgot. I plugged the lights into the socket operated by this switch."

"You should have had an electrician do it," he said teasingly. "Nice tree."

"Thank you."

"The old-fashioned kind."

Leaving her standing just inside the door, he walked over to the fireplace. Glowing red coals were still smoldering beneath a stack of charred wood. He moved the screen aside, stirred the coals with a poker, and added two new logs. They caught immediately.

In the bright firelight, the melting snowflakes on his hair and shoulders sparkled like diamonds. He turned and looked at Ria. His eyes, his shadowed face, the purposeful way he moved toward her, made her tremble.

"I'll put the coffee on," she said breathlessly.

He caught her hand as she went past him. "Ria?"

"What?"

"There's snow on your hair," he whispered. She shook her head. He watched the sensuous movement of her loose hair. "It's beautiful. Black as midnight. So shiny and silky. So seductive."

What was seductive, she thought, was the way he threaded his fingers through it and spread it out on the fur shoulders of her coat. His eyes moved over her face, down her throat, into the shadowy cleft between her breasts. Ria shivered, and said, "It'll be warm in just a minute."

"Baby, it's already warm."

His voice reminded her of the low purring of his car's engine. The power behind it was temperately held in check. One careless move and it could zoom out of control.

Stepping closer, he cupped her face between his hands and stroked her cold cheeks with his thumbs, warming them instantly. He bent his head and brushed his lips across hers.

His first kiss was light and questing. The next one was firm and questing. Ria gasped and quickly turned her head away. "I'm sorry," he said. "I had no right to do that. It's just that . . . damn, I wanted to kiss you."

She lifted her face up to his again. She felt boneless, as light as air. Her eyes remained open only because they were greedy to look at him. "Don't apologize. This is Christmas Eve."

"In that case . . ."

He kissed her again. This time his mouth opened over her lips, urging them to part. She complied. They tasted each other. Their tongues touched. Circuit completed. Nerve endings popped and hissed like live wires.

"You were right, Ria," he said in a raspy tone of voice, moving his lips against her dewy mouth. "There's nothing like the real thing."

He pulled her against him. His hands caressed her through the lavish fur of her coat. Then he flung it aside, twirling it out and away from her like a matador's cape. It landed on the couch, a few feet away. His eager and curious hands moved over her. They explored the shallow valley of her spine, her hips, her thighs—the backs, sides, and front of them.

She made a startled sound when he splayed his hand over her lower body. Taylor didn't remove his hand, though he raised his head and looked down into her face with an unspoken question in his eyes. She was panting through parted, moist lips. Her eyelids fluttered open, and she gazed up at him. Then she tilted her body forward, filling the hollow of his palm with her mound.

They both groaned with the delicious pain of desire. He stroked her, petted her, pressed her, seeking the source of her heat. While kissing madly, he shrugged out of his suit coat. Ria thought that there must have been at least a thousand buttons on his vest, but at last they were all undone and her hands were caressing his chest through his white silk shirt.

He laid his hands on her shoulders and slowly pushed down her dress. His fingertips skated down her throat and over her collarbone. She threw her head back and he kissed her neck. His mouth was open, hot, fiercely possessive.

Ria fumbled with the buttons of his shirt after having pulled it from his waistband. When they were all undone, her fingers combed through his generous chest hair. She reveled in the shape of his form and the vibrancy of his skin.

Reaching around her, he slid down the back zipper of her dress. The bodice dropped to her waist. She wasn't wearing anything underneath. Reflexively she raised her hands to cover herself, but he gently drew her hands away.

"No, please," he whispered. "You're beautiful."

Entranced, he watched the fluid movement of her breasts as she withdrew her arms from her tight sleeves. He touched her so lightly that he was barely touching her at all as he framed her breasts between his hands. Then he slid his hands up the undersides of her arms all the way to her wrists. He raised her hands and folded them together around his neck.

He held her close, skin to skin. For a moment that was enough. But then their mutual sighs of pleasure became ragged with need. He caressed her breasts, deftly fingering the nipples. He lifted one to his mouth. His lips enclosed it. His rough, damp tongue finessed it into a tight little peak. He murmured something about sucking it before he matched action to words.

Desire pumped through Ria with every tugging motion of his mouth. When he unfastened her belt and eased her dress over her hips, her only protest was that he didn't do it quickly enough. The sequin dress pooled around her feet and she stepped out of the glittering heap wearing only a black garter belt, black panties, and sooty stockings with her high heels.

Taylor swore softly. "Santa Claus must think I've been very, very good." He buried all ten fingers in her cloud of black hair and seared her mouth with a long, tongue-thrusting kiss. Lifting her against him, he carried her to the couch. As he watched her recline on top of the fur coat, he stripped off his clothing. Naked and marvelously virile, he levered himself down beside her.

"It's no secret that I want you." He slipped his hand into her panties. "Do you want me, Ria?" Her body said yes. His fingers sank into a wealth of creaminess. But he wanted to hear the words coming from her beautiful, sexy mouth. "Tell me."

"Yes, I want you."

He moved between her thighs. She looped her arms around his neck. Their lips met just as his sex, hard and smooth and full, tunneled deep inside her.

Two

"How did this happen?" Taylor's dark brows were pulled together, creating a cleft between them.

"Didn't your father ever have a man-to-man talk with you about the birds and the bees?" Ria asked sweetly. That cleft grew deeper in proportion to his scowl. "If so, you should know how this happened."

It had been only minutes since Ria Lavender had walked through the door of Taylor's office and delivered her stunning news. It seemed like eons. The tension between them had mounted, layer upon layer, like the formation of a volcanic mountain.

"I meant, why weren't you protected?" He pushed the words through his teeth, which formed a formidable white barrier behind his tight lips.

"Why weren't you?"

"Usually I am. I read the papers, I heed the warnings."

"You slipped up, I guess."

"I took it for granted that any reasonably intelligent woman who is sexually active in this age of sexual liberation would practice some means of contraception."

Ria's green eyes narrowed. "One," she said, holding up a perfectly manicured index finger, "I'm not sexually active in the way you suggest. I don't know what happened to me Christmas Eve. Probably too much champagne. But I'm not in the habit of taking strangers home to bed with me, and I resent your implication that I am.

"Two." The next finger joined its sister and formed a twin spire pointing ceilingward. "I care too much about my general health to risk it by taking oral contraceptives. And three"—the third finger sprang up—"don't ever take anything concerning me for granted."

Cursing, Taylor left his desk and moved to the windows behind it. Cramming his fists into his pockets and hunching his shoulders, he glowered at her. Pregnancy wasn't the only trap she'd sprung on him. One sight of her and he was back on that sofa, listening to those quick, light little breaths she'd drawn when she came. He wished he could block out that disturbing sound. He wished his nose would forget the tantalizing mixture of smells—fresh Christmas tree, fireplace smoke, scented woman flesh, and sex.

It had been eight weeks, yet he vividly remembered how she'd felt entwined with him beneath the fur coat he'd pulled over them before they fell asleep. The cavemen had had something there, sleeping naked with their mates under piles of fur. It was a custom homo sapiens should have clung to.

Today Ria Lavender was all trussed up in a practical navy business suit trimmed with brass buttons and red piping. Taylor couldn't help but wonder if beneath that suit she was wearing crotch-teasing undies like the ones she'd been wearing Christmas Eve. He'd bet his newly won mayor's office that her skin was as warm and satiny as it had been then. And even though her hair was pulled back into a neat, professional knot, he could almost feel it sliding between his fingers, each long strand as luxurious as a black velvet ribbon.

He'd actually been glad to hear from her. Like a dumb kid who had scored with a woman for the first time, he'd been almost giddy when his secretary had buzzed him to say that Ms. Ria Lavender had arrived for their appointment.

Yes, he'd been looking forward to this meeting, curious as to why she'd contacted him, hoping that it wasn't strictly business. He'd quailed his optimism by thinking that maybe she wanted his company's bid to do the wiring on a project of hers. Still, he hadn't been able to suppress his excitement.

Then she'd hit him between the eyes with, "I'm pregnant."

It just wasn't possible. Situations like this didn't happen to grown men. To stupid, pimply kids, yes, but not to mayors-elect. This was either her poor idea of a joke or a damning accusation.

He looked at her suspiciously. Just what was this broad up to? He wasn't sure yet. For the time being he'd play devil's advocate and try to find out.

"Are you sure you're pregnant?"

Impatiently Ria recrossed her silk-sheathed legs. "Yes."

"Based on a late period?"

"Based on a reliable scientific method of determination administered in my gynecologist's office yesterday morning," she replied tetchily. "I'm pregnant, Mr. MacKensie, and you're the father."

He smirked skeptically. "Funny how we met, isn't it?"

The question startled her. "That's what cocktail

parties are for, for people to meet. What has how we met got to do with this?"

"Maybe nothing. Maybe everything."

"I wish you'd get to the point."

"All right," he said, coming around to face her. "I made a lot of enemies in this recent election. They were determined to see me defeated. I wasn't. I won. But the swearing in is still a few months away. Let's say, for the sake of argument, that my enemies are looking for a way to discredit me. Where am I most vulnerable?"

"Are you always this paranoid?"

He ignored her and continued his train of thought. "I'm single. Bleeker has been married to the same woman for thirty-some-odd years and has eight children and fifteen grandchildren. He looks as folksy, established, and credible as Mr. Rogers. Nobody even thought of prying into his private life during the campaign.

"I, on the other hand, am thirty years younger and unmarried. I take a woman out to dinner and *bingo*"—he slapped his hands together—"everybody starts speculating on what we do together in bed."

Ria whisked a piece of nonexistent lint off her skirt and theatrically glanced at her watch. "I suppose all this is leading up to something. If not, I think it's fair to tell you that I'm only interested in what you did in bed with me, and only then because it resulted in a baby."

"I'm leading up to something, all right." He sat down on the corner of his desk. One Italian-leather-shod foot was planted in the maroon carpet; the other swung idly back and forth. He folded his hands over his knee, leaned forward and down, and took a bead on Ria's green eyes—which he couldn't help but notice were rimmed with incredibly long, curly, dark lashes. "I don't think our meeting was an accident, Ms. Lavender. I think you were paid by my enemies to compromise me in the worst possible way."

"Are you insane?"

"That's it, isn't it?"

She shook her head in disbelief. "You *won*, you fool. If this was a political plot, it failed the minute the returns came in."

"I haven't assumed office yet. What better way to ruin me than to produce a pregnant woman claiming that I'm the father of her child? Bleeker would demand a—" He broke off when Ria started laughing.

"If I were a saboteur, which I most certainly am *not*, I would have done something that wasn't so hard on myself, something that didn't make me heave my breakfast into the toilet bowl every morning and make me so tired in the evenings that brushing my hair seems like an insurmountable task."

Ria became angrier by the second as the implications of his accusation began to soak in. "I didn't want this to happen any more than you did. It's going to be extremely inconvenient for me to have a baby right now. I have a career, Mr. MacKensie. I'm a well-established architect, with a heavy work schedule mapped out for the next several months."

"Tough luck. That only reenforces my argument for contraception. If you're going to screw around, you ought to practice some method of birth control."

Her face was white with fury. "I do not screw around."

"Oh, yeah? Well, my experience with you says otherwise. What'd you do, draw my name out of a hat? Did I get the short straw? Is that how you arrived at daddyo's name?"

"You creep."

"What do you expect from me? To fall all over myself thanking you for having my baby?"

"Are you going to hear me out or not?"

"I'm not." He pointed down at her stomach and shouted angrily, "Yankee Doodle Dandy could be the father of your kid, for all I know."

Ria tucked her purse under her arm and rose from her chair with regal composure. She turned on the heels of her red pumps and walked to the door. There she faced him again, her hand on the doorknob. "I wish Yankee Doodle Dandy were. Anyone, in fact, but you."

"May I come in?" he asked politely. If he had had a hat, it would have been in hand.

"No."

"Please?"

"Why?"

"I want to talk to you."

"And hurl more ugly accusations? No, thank you, Mr. MacKensie." Ria started to close the door. He stuck out his hand and caught it.

Ria looked at him closely. What she saw made her feel better. If his appearance was any indication, he'd had a hellish day. His dark hair was mussed. His tie had been loosened and the collar button on his shirt undone. He was holding his suit coat over his shoulder by the crook of his finger. He looked haggard and worried and tired. For a man who had gone through a heated campaign with nary a wrinkle, his dishevelment was a dead giveaway that he'd suffered some recent mental anguish.

Too bad, Ria thought. She refused to be moved to pity, not after the things he'd said to her. "Just go away and leave me alone. Forget everything I said this morning."

"I can't."

"I never should have told you."

"Of course you should have."

Annoyed, she shifted her weight from one foot to the other, while still blocking his entrance. "Need I remind you, Mr. MacKensie, that you didn't take the news too well? You were insulting and abusive."

"That's one of the reasons I'm here, to apologize for my knee-jerk reaction. Grant me one point."

"What?" she asked cautiously.

"That my initial reaction was just a teensy bit justified."

His eyes were intensely blue. They were set off by his dark hair and tanned face. Wary of their persuasiveness, Ria lowered her gaze to his vest. But that, too, evoked memories. Was it really possible that she had once unbuttoned his vest in a lustful hurry to touch him? Had her fingers fumbled in their rush to gain access to him? She couldn't imagine reaching out to touch him now.

She cleared her throat uneasily. Reasoning that she owed him the courtesy of accepting his apology, she decided to be conciliatory. "I suppose that what I had to tell you did come as quite a shock."

"Then will you please let me come in, Ria?"

Maybe it was because he addressed her by name. She couldn't explain it to herself afterward. But for whatever reason, she stepped aside. He came in. She closed the door behind him and they were alone.

The room had changed. It was filled with golden afternoon sunlight rather than flickering firelight. The fireplace had been cleaned out and a potted philodendron with leaves as large and flat as placemats stood in front of the brass screen. A leafy ficus occupied the spot where the Christmas tree had been.

"You have a green thumb," he remarked.

She inclined her head in acknowledgment of the compliment and indicated a chair. She sat down in a bentwood rocker. Both of them avoided the sofa, looking past it as though it weren't there. The room might have changed with the season, but the atmosphere still teemed with vivid and disturbing memories of a snowy night.

"Would you like something to drink?"

"Not if that's all you've got." He nodded toward the glass sitting on the end table beside the rocker. "What is that?"

"Alka-Seltzer."

"Are you sick?"

"I get indigestion every afternoon."

"Oh."

"I can get you a soft drink," Ria offered. "Or something stronger."

"No, thanks."

A clock was ticking. It seemed very loud. The rocker squeaked slightly each time it moved to and fro. Whenever their eyes accidentally met, they guiltily looked away, like children who'd been caught playing doctor the day before.

Ria wished she hadn't changed out of her tailored suit and into the old jeans and T-shirt. She wished she had on a brassiere. She wished she had on shoes. She knew that she needed to take a firm stand with this man. Bare feet weren't a very reassuring platform. Her hair was a mess. After taking down her bun, she'd only shaken it out. It hung unbrushed and untamed around her shoulders.

She knew the strain of the last twenty-four hours was evident on her face. She hadn't been able to hold down much food lately. Her cheeks were gaunt. No amount of Erase would hide the violet crescents beneath her eyes. She hadn't slept at all the night before, worrying over her dilemma and planning what she was going to say to Councilman MacKensie the next morning.

In the end she had decided to take the straightforward, honest approach. And just look what honesty had gotten her. His temper. His suspicion. His contempt.

"How long have you lived here?"

She roused herself to answer his conversational question. "Going on three years. Ever since I started working at Bishop and Harvey."

"It's a nice house."

"Thank you."

"Cozy."

"Uh-huh."

"Did you decorate it yourself?"

"Yes."

"This is a good neighborhood."

"The city keeps the garbage picked up and the streets repaired," she said, smiling sickly.

"Ah, well, that's good to hear." His smile was just as puny as hers. "It felt almost like spring today."

"Yes. I saw some daffodils already in bloom."

Sitting on the edge of his chair, his knees widespread, Taylor stared at the hardwood floor between his feet. The fingers of one hand were nervously doing push-ups against the fingers of the other. He forced a cough. "When, uh, when did you know about, uh, the, uh, baby?"

From all she'd read, heard, and experienced firsthand about Taylor MacKensie, stuttering was totally out of character. His voice frequently rang out in the City Council chambers as he waxed eloquently and intelligently on the topics presented for the council's review. His campaign speeches had been incisive, amusing, and articulate. Reporters' questions, even the most probing or complex, never left him at a loss for words.

It was gratifying to know that he was as uneasy now as she had been that morning before entering his office. Diving off the cliffs at Acapulco couldn't compare to how she'd felt when she'd walked through that door and faced him for the first time since Christmas morning. Especially in light of what she had to tell him.

"When did I know?" Ria kept her eyes averted. "I missed a period."

He fidgeted on the edge of his seat. "I understand that happens sometimes."

"It does. But never to me. I'm always like clockwork."

This time it was she who coughed. It flustered her to talk about such personal things to this stranger. Well, not exactly "stranger." Yes, this stranger. What did she really know about him? That he was handsome. That he knew how to open a bottle of champagne correctly. That he was a good driver on snowy streets. That he could charm the pants off a woman. Literally.

She began again. "I started feeling sick . . . not really sick, just . . ." She foundered, looking for a word that precisely described that bloated feeling, that lassitude, that inability to draw enough breath, that feeling of being full to bursting even when she was hungry. There wasn't a word descriptive enough. "There were just symptoms," she said conclusively.

"Like what?"

"Upset stomach. Emotional instability. Itchy—"

He cocked his head inquisitively. "Itchy . . . ?"

"Breasts," she supplied huskily, having to force the word through her lips.

"Oh." He looked down at her chest and kept looking in that vicinity for a long, uncomfortable time. "I'm sorry."

She crossed her arms over her stomach, wishing she could place her hands over her breasts to shield her hardening nipples from his piercing eyes. "You know the symptoms," she said shortly.

Taylor looked completely baffled. "Yeah, I guess."

"Then I skipped another period last month. I finally went to the doctor yesterday, and he confirmed my own diagnosis. My due date is September twenty-sixth."

He expulsed a deep breath. The jury had just brought in a guilty verdict. "I guess that cinches it."

"There was never any doubt about the child's father, despite what you might think of my sex life, Mr. MacKensie."

"Make it Taylor, okay?" he demanded crossly.

Just as crossly she said, "Regardless of your 'experience' with me, as you so ungallantly referred to it, I don't sleep around."

"Forgive me for saying that. I shouldn't have."

Her angry outburst had exhausted her. Her shoulders slumped, and she rested her head on the caned back of her chair. "I suppose you had every right to think that." Her soft laugh was bitter and self-disparaging. "On Christmas Eve, I was an easy lay."

"Don't say that."

"Well, wasn't I?" She raised her head and looked at him directly.

"I never thought that. Then or now."

"You thought that this morning."

He ran a weary hand down his face and blew out another gust of carbon dioxide. "We're going in circles and getting nowhere." He held her gaze for a moment. "Look, I don't think you're an easy lay. Because if you are, then I am. And I'm more discriminating than your average tomcat.

"So let's just drop whatever recriminations we're harboring, self-imposed or otherwise, and try to figure out what we're going to do about the consequences, okay?" Ria only nodded. "What about this guy you told me you're seeing? The one with the elderly mother in Florida."

"Funny, Guy happens to be his name." She was surprised that he remembered the details. "Guy Patterson. He's an associate in the firm."

"Have you told him yet?"

"Yes. As soon as I'd told you. I felt I owed him that."

"And?"

Guy Patterson had taken the news of her pregnancy no better than Taylor had. Worse, in fact. He'd been livid, calling her in explicit terms the names Taylor had only implied.

"He's permanently out of the picture," she said without elaboration.

Actually, having Guy out of her life was a relief. Older by fifteen years, he was somewhat stuffy. She was tired of his staid, conservative ideas. Their conversations were boring, because he directed them to topics only he was interested in. When you got right down to it, Guy was a persnickety old maid, and not much fun to be around. The only reason she was dating him was that nobody better had come on the scene. She wouldn't have chosen this earth-shattering way to break it off with him, but she was glad it had been done so irrevocably.

"You could have passed the child off as his," Taylor said tentatively. "Why didn't you?"

"I never would have done that," Ria exclaimed, taking umbrage. "What kind of woman do you think I am?"

"All right, I'm sorry."

"Besides, I couldn't have deceived him even if I'd wanted to. Guy had a vasectomy years ago."

He'd made no secret of it. When their relationship had developed into more than that of working associates, he'd told Ria that he might consider marriage, but children were out of the question. There was another reason why Guy couldn't possibly be the father of her baby, but she'd let Mr. MacKensie think what he would.

"Has this ever happened to you?" she asked suddenly.

"You mean fathering a child? No. How 'bout you? Have you ever been pregnant?"

"No." She wondered why she was pleased to know that this was new to him too. There was no explanation except that she would have hated knowing she was one of a group of unfortunates. Taylor's Tarnished.

He studied her carefully for a moment, but lowered his eyes before asking, "Did you come to me for financial assistance?"

"Financial assistance for what?"

"Any number of things."

"Like . . . ?"

"Abortion. Is that what you plan to do?"

Ria turned her head, giving him her profile. Tears were glistening in her eyes. They reflected the light of the setting sun coming through the window.

"No. Mr. Mac— No, Taylor. I believe in living with my mistakes, not burying them. And for your information, abortions come cheap these days."

"I was only asking because the timing is right. I know there's a deadline before that, uh, solution becomes unfeasible."

"Are you sure you're not suggesting that's what I should do? Before you answer, I should warn you that that's a rhetorical question. I won't be having an abortion." She turned her head and looked at him squarely, almost defiantly. "Why else do you think I'd come to you for money?"

"To help with supporting the child, before and after it's born."

"I earn a very good salary, in addition to the commission I make on each job. Thank you very much, but I don't need your money, Mr. Mac-Kensie." Leaving her chair, she picked up the Alka-Seltzer-coated glass on the end table and made a beeline for the door across the room.

Taylor followed her. Her kitchen was alive with a jungle of plants. He had to swat aside a leaf as he went in. She was rinsing out the glass in a stainless-steel sink.

"Why do you bristle at everything I say?"

She swung around to face him. "Because I find everything you say offensive."

"Well, pardon me, ma'am, but I'm not quite myself today." His tone of voice bordered on loud. "Forgive me for pointing out that we're a little old to be caught 'in trouble' like a couple of teenagers. This didn't happen in the back of Dad's Ford after the prom."

"That's why I don't see why we can't be adult about it and stop throwing blame on each other."

"We can. But the idea of a baby is going to take some getting used to. You've had weeks to reckon with it. It's new to me. Don't expect me to be my normal, glib self today. I've suffered a shock."

"So have I!" she yelled back. "It's not your body that is going through all these changes, it's mine. Think about the adjustments I've had to make."

"I can appreciate that," he said, striving for calm.

"You have a damn funny way of showing it."

"I said I was sorry."

"Then stop making unflattering innuendos about my milking you for money, etcetera. I'm willing to live up to my obligation. Why aren't you? We share this responsibility equally. We were both on that couch. We both enjoyed it. It was a simultaneous—"

Horrified at what she heard herself saying, Ria turned her back on him again. Her cheeks were on fire. She hadn't blushed before or since Christmas Eve. It seemed that she'd packed a lifetime of blushes away and saved them all for Taylor MacKensie.

Her heart was thudding. Her mouth was dry and her palms were wet. In her ears she heard a roar as loud as crashing waves. In fact, it felt as though they were ebbing and flowing through her burning earlobes.

It took a moment for her to collect herself. "All I meant is that I'm willing to assume responsibility for my actions that night," she said in a shaky voice. "It's not going to be easy for me to have a baby, but I am and that's that. You don't know me very well or you never could have thought I'd have an abortion." She shuddered.

"Why did you bother to tell me about the baby at all?"

She came around slowly, clearly mystified by his question. "You didn't want to know that you had fathered a child? I considered it my moral obligation to tell you."

"Your integrity is admirable."

"But you'd just as soon I hadn't involved you," she said with a humorless laugh. "Won't the ski bunny like it?"

"The ski bunny?"

"The woman who got ticked off when you didn't go on the ski trip with her."

"Lisa?"

Lisa. Ria had wondered later what Lisa would have thought of Taylor's Christmas Eve. Would

she have been jealous? Or had she been making it
with a ski instructor at the same time? Were they
sophisticated enough to tell each other about their
escapades? Had he regaled Lisa with a detailed
account of their lovemaking, perhaps for the purpose of stimulating her?

The thought made Ria ill. She pressed one hand
against her stomach and covered her mouth with
the other.

Taylor jumped as if he'd been shot. "What's the
matter?"

"Nothing."

"Something, dammit."

"Nothing!"

"You're green!"

She drew a deep breath through chalky lips.
"I'm a little queasy, that's all."

"Sit down." He yanked a chair away from the
table.

"I'm fine, really."

"Sit down." The order was issued in a terse,
authoritarian voice that Ria was too weak and
woozy to argue with. He pulled out a chair for
himself and dropped down into it, plowing his
hands through his hair and cursing. "Don't scare
me like that again. Can I get you something?"

"No." She glanced up at him. He was glaring at
her sternly. "All right. A cracker. That helps settle
my stomach sometimes."

She told him where he could find a box of saltines in the pantry. He shook crumbs all over the
table as he wrestled two crackers out of their
cellophane package. The box fell to the floor when
he bumped the edge of the table with his thigh as
he sat back down. Nibbling the cracker, Ria began to laugh.

"What?" he grumbled.

"For a man who's so adept at uncorking champagne, you don't handle saltines very well."

He smiled with chagrin. "Well, I've had more practice with champagne than with pregnant ladies."

Ria sobered instantly. She dusted salt off her hands as she said softly, "I'm sure you have."

It surprised them both when he reached across the table and covered her hands with his. "Please don't take offense," he said. "I didn't mean anything by it."

She stared at his hand. It was a beautifully masculine hand. Blunt, well-trimmed fingernails. Her stomach experienced a sinking sensation when she remembered those very hands moving over her body, massaging the breasts that even now ached to be touched. Those fingertips had stroked the secret-most part of her body, lifting her toward ecstasy, taking and giving pleasure in equal quantity. At least she thought he'd taken pleasure in caressing her. She hoped so.

Discomfited by her thoughts, she brought her head up and looked straight into his blue eyes. "Did you tell Lisa about me?"

"Of course not." He abruptly withdrew his hand from hers.

"I don't think I could have stood that." She felt weepy, as she had in the last several weeks, and hoped to heaven she didn't burst into tears over the thought of him and Lisa having a good laugh at her expense.

"I'll confess to going out with a lot of women, but I'm not a complete jerk, Ria."

"I thought you might have used Christmas Eve to make Lisa jealous."

"Did you use it to make Guy jealous?"

"I don't play games like that."

"Neither do I."

She saw that he was telling her the truth. "I didn't tell anybody."

"You had to tell Guy when you told him about the baby."

"I wasn't specific about the date. I didn't name you. Are you still seeing her?"

"Lisa? Yes."

"What will she think of the situation?"

"It isn't any of her business."

Ria stared at him, aghast. "She may beg to differ."

"It isn't like that between us."

He'd felt free to take another woman to bed on Christmas Eve without having to grapple about it later with either his conscience or his steady lady friend. That typified more than anything what a casual, forgettable event their lovemaking had been for him. Ria's heart was aching around the edges, as though the border of her soul had been trespassed.

"Now that we've acknowledged our dual responsibility for this child," he said, "and eliminated abortion as an alternative, what do you suggest we do?"

Ria steadily held his gaze. "You're going to marry me, Mr. MacKensie."

Three

After a long, tense silence, he said, "Well, that answers that." '

"I see no need to beat around the bush."

"Ms. Lavender, I doubt if you've ever beat around the bush." He left his chair and went to the refrigerator. Finding a beer inside, he opened it. "Since you've proposed, I feel at liberty to drink one of your beers."

"Help yourself."

"Thank you." He mockingly saluted her with the can, then sipped from it, eyeing her over the top of it. "Apparently our perspectives on Christmas Eve vary slightly."

"What do you mean?"

"By no stretch of the imagination were you forced, or even coerced. You were just as willing to stretch out naked on that fur coat as I was."

"You don't have to get vulgar."

"And you don't have to get sanctimonious."

"I only wanted you to understand what I expect from you."

He forcibly tamped down his temper and said in

a more reasonable tone, "You think we should get married, huh? Give me one good reason."

"As you just said, we were both willing to . . ." She glanced away, then, not wanting him to mistake her embarrassment for weakness, looked him straight in the eye. "Why should I shoulder this responsibility alone?"

"Don't you read *Good Housekeeping* and *Cosmopolitan*? It's fashionable for single parents, men included, to rear children."

"I intend to rear the child alone."

He raised the beer can close to his face and studied it. "This must be strong stuff. For a minute there I thought you had proposed marriage, and then in the next breath said you planned to rear the baby by yourself."

"This isn't a joke!"

"You're damn right it's not. So would you please stop talking in riddles?" He slammed the can down on the counter top. "Which is it, Ria? Do we marry or do you remain a single mother?"

"Both. I don't care if we get an annulment the minute I leave the hospital. But my baby is going to be legitimate and have both parents there the day he's born."

"If you want an annulment immediately afterward, then why bother going through the formalities?"

She stared at him with incredulity. "Is that asking too much?"

"No, dammit. That's not what I meant." He pointed a finger toward her lap. "Do you think I'd turn my back on my child? Not care anything about him?"

"I don't know. I don't know you."

"Obviously not." He stopped shouting, threw his head back, and drew a deep breath. "I was only trying to understand why you think we should get married, when what you really want is to rear the child by yourself."

Ria left her chair and started fiddling with the blinds on the window. "Call it an old-fashioned quirk of mine."

"Like natural Christmas trees."

She glanced at him quickly over her shoulder. "Yes. Like that. Parents should be married when their child is born."

Taylor came up behind her and laid his hands on her shoulders. He turned her around and tilted her head back. Ria held herself stiffly. This seemingly innocuous embrace was too reminiscent of when he had told her there was snow in her hair and then tilted her head back for their first kiss. He was wearing the same tender expression.

"Try again, Ria. Tell me why you want us to get married. Religious convictions?"

"Partially, but not entirely."

"Have you told your parents about the baby? Are they pressuring you?"

"No on both accounts."

"Then why? This is the reason you came to my office today, isn't it? To ask me to marry you."

"To insist that you do."

"Don't you think I deserve to know the reason behind that insistence?" She tried to work herself out of his grasp, but he wouldn't allow it. "Tell me, Ria."

"It doesn't matter."

"The hell it doesn't."

"Look, Taylor, I know you don't love me. I don't love you. We're not 'in love.' I'm not sure we even like each other. What happened between us was purely physical. Spontaneous combustion of the glands. It was . . ." She wet her lips nervously. "Lust."

His eyes glowed hotly. "Agreed."

"And now we're paying for it."

"Maybe."

"But I don't think the child should have to."

"Nor do I."

"So for his sake—"

"Cut the crap," he interrupted impatiently. "Why should we get married?"

"I've already told—"

"*Why?*"

"Because I was born illegitimate."

Angrily pushing herself away from him, she stamped back into the living room. Feeling cornered, she spun around to face him when she heard his footsteps behind her. "There. Satisfied? I don't want my child to grow up with the stigma that I had."

"You seem to have turned out okay," he said quietly.

"Thanks to two wonderful people who adopted me. Don't worry, the mother of your child is not a psychopath. I don't have any life-threatening hang-ups. I grew up secure in the knowledge that I was loved and wanted by Robert and Frida Lavender."

"Some kids who are reared by their natural parents aren't that lucky."

"I know that," Ria said, wringing her hands. "I thank God for Mom and Dad." She drew a shuddering breath. "But I never got over knowing that someone didn't want me. Two people gave me away, discarded me, because I was a biological accident. They didn't want to make a baby together." She avoided looking at him. "Just as we didn't."

Taylor crossed the room and took her hand. Dragging her along behind him, he moved to the couch and pulled her down beside him. "You look exhausted. Sit down."

"I mean it, Taylor." There was a desperate edge to her voice. "I won't do that to my baby."

"I hear you."

Now that the truth was out, Ria let her guard down. She laid her head on the back of the couch. She pulled in one of those insufficient deep breaths and let it out slowly, willing her body to relax.

As it did nearly every evening now, a drowsiness stole over her. She could barely keep her eyes open. Several minutes passed before she realized that they were actually closed. When she opened them, Taylor was watching her. He was smiling.

"What's the matter?"

He said, "I was just thinking about how first impressions can fool you." Her inquisitive gaze prompted him to elaborate. "When I first saw you, I was staggered by how beautiful you are."

She swallowed with difficulty. "Thank you."

He shrugged. "No sense in pretending now that I didn't like what I saw. You know better." Their eyes held for an uncomfortably long time. Finally he continued. "I thought you were a really classy lady. The way you dressed. The way you flirted. You had a great pair of tits, a terrific ass, and a wonderful sense of humor."

Her sense of humor came through for her now. Ria, blushing, laughed self-consciously. "Thanks again, though I want it to go on record that I oppose your sexist estimation."

"Consider it recorded."

"Maybe you'd better make your point, Mr. Mac-Kensie."

He was staring at the base of her neck the way a penniless boy stares at the chocolate cake in the bakery window. "Yeah, maybe I'd better," he said gruffly. "My point is that under that sophisticated veneer, Ria Lavender is an old-fashioned girl at heart. She clings to a quaint, outdated code of morality."

"Are you making fun of me?"

"No. Complimenting you. Women with such high standards are hard to come by these days."

"They are not," she retorted crisply. "You've just never looked for them."

He had the grace to laugh. "Guilty. But I do have some redeeming qualities. If you'd given me half a chance, I would have proposed to you first."

Her lips parted in astonishment.

"That's right, Ria," he said, tucking a strand of hair behind her ear. "I came here tonight to ask you to marry me. At least until the child is born."

"Why?"

He looked startled, then laughed. "For all the reasons you cited. I believe you mentioned something about living with one's mistakes, about sharing responsibility, legitimacy."

"If you agreed with everything, why did you put me on the defensive?"

"You told me yourself on Christmas Eve that you doubted I'd ever let anybody bully me. When you started making demands, I started defying you."

"So I went through all those explanations for nothing."

"I don't think it was wasted. I know you better now, what you think and how you feel about things."

"Well, you're still a mystery to me."

"Let me clear up one vital point." When he had her full attention he said, "You obviously think I'm an indiscriminate stud, who wouldn't have any qualms about populating the state with little bastard MacKensies." He smiled when she lowered her eyes guiltily. "On the contrary, I have a conscience and a strong moral fiber. If this had happened to me when I was in high school, I would have done the honorable thing and married the girl."

That made Ria angry. "I don't need or want your pity."

"Damn, you're prickly. Don't start another argument. Not when I've just got you calmed down."

"And don't refer to me as if I were a high-strung mare."

He cursed. "Can we go back to the subject, please?"

She regained control of her temper. "I wasn't thinking of me when I asked you to marry me. I was thinking only of the child."

"So am I," Taylor argued. "He's mine too. I have a vested interest in his future. I'd never relinquish all legal claims to him. Which might very well happen if we weren't married."

"So you're doing it for legal purposes."

"We both have our reasons."

Deep in thought, Ria contemplated her bare toes. She supposed it was only fair that he have some legal rights to the child. Her life would have been terribly empty without Robert Lavender in it. Could she selfishly deny her baby its father? Even a part-time father?

"All right. We'll work out some sort of mutual custody agreement with the annulment."

"Here we are talking about the annulment and we haven't even discussed the wedding yet."

She returned his smile. "There's plenty of time for that. All I ask is that we be married a week or so before my due date."

She started to stand, thinking that an agreement had been reached. Taylor's hand shot out and grabbed a handful of T-shirt. "I have one condition."

As she sat back down, Ria regarded him suspiciously. "What?"

"We marry right away. Tomorrow. The day after, at least. As soon as possible."

"Why the rush?"

"Because it would be politically disastrous for me to rush out and get married a few days before my child is born."

"But you'll already be in office. Not Bleeker, not anybody else, can hurt you at that point."

"I'll be in office, yes, but how effective can I be if my morality is on the line?" He was shaking his head. "Uh-uh. We've got to be married long before the baby is born."

"No one will ever have to know that you're the father. I won't tell anybody. We'll go out of town to get married. You can see the baby on the sly."

"Ria, both of us have a high public profile. You know a lot of people. So do I. Many of them saw us leave that party together on Christmas Eve."

"Do you really think they'd put two and two together?"

"No, they'd add up one and one and get three. You, me, and baby. Or count up nine months from Christmas Eve and get September twenty-sixth. And I detest sneakiness. If we're doing this to legitimize our child, then we'd better do it right away. Otherwise, we'd do just as well not getting married at all."

"But everyone will know why we got married if we get an annulment as soon as the baby is born."

"It will be pure speculation."

"There'll be speculation aplenty if we rush right out and get married without even dating first. Rumors will really start flying when I begin to show."

He glanced down at her flat tummy. Impulsively he laid his hand on it. "Hard to believe, isn't it? That there's really a baby in there?"

It was hard for Ria to believe that her bones could turn to butter whenever he touched her. But with his palm lying firm and warm on her lower abdomen, she was afflicted with a languor and light-headedness that had nothing to do with pregnancy.

"Now that I've had time to think about it, I kinda like the idea of my baby growing inside you." He lifted those startling blue eyes up to hers. "In fact, I like the idea of you, period."

He leaned forward and placed a solid kiss on her lips. Then, tilting his head to one side, he kissed her again. This time his lips were parted. They pressed against hers, rubbing them slightly until they, too, separated.

She hadn't been inebriated on Christmas Eve after all. His kisses hadn't been embellished by the magic of champagne or by her memory. They were just as skillful and sinful as she had remembered. His tongue was nimble and quick and light, slow and sleek and sexy.

His hand moved up to the side of her breast and pressed the fullness. He swept his thumb across her nipple and Ria moaned because the caress felt so good to the tender, achy, itchy flesh.

He sighed her name as the kiss intensified. He applied more pressure to her mouth, and his tongue delved deeper. Ria became lost in the wonder of his kiss, in the solid presence of his strong body, in the smell of his skin and hair. She became immersed again in Taylor MacKensie, just as she had on Christmas Eve. And she was drowning, drowning. . . .

Ria pulled herself up sharply. "No. Taylor, we can't."

He was breathing hard, blinking rapidly. "How come?"

"Because."

"Good reason."

"I have a condition of my own. There can't be any intimacy between us."

"I wish you'd told me that about three kisses and one feel ago," he muttered.

She stood up and pulled down her T-shirt, which had become twisted up beneath her breasts. She ran her fingers through her hair in a futile attempt to straighten it. She smoothed her hands down the front of her thighs, wishing that would cool the sweet fever burning between them. Why did she still want him? How could she still want him, when she was paying so dearly for their one night together? "Any kind of emotional or physical involvement between us will only make it harder."

"It couldn't possibly get any harder than it is right now."

"Taylor!"

"Just kidding." Slowly and awkwardly he came to his feet. "I'll make all the arrangements and call you." He headed for the door.

"Wait! You can't leave before we discuss this. What are we going to say when people ask why we're not living together?"

"They won't ask. We will be living together."

"What? We can't! Where?"

"My house."

"Out of the question."

"Ria, believe me, I'm in no condition for a debate right now."

"We've got to get this settled."

"And I've got to get this settled," he shouted, pointing downward. Her mouth clicked shut. He nodded. "Right. I've got to go home, take a cold shower, and try to reconcile myself to being married in name only to a beautiful, sexy, pregnant lady. Okay?" he asked crossly. "I'll call you."

"Ready?"

"Yes."

Taylor nodded at her approvingly and ushered her into the judge's chambers. He'd handled all the details and arranged for the judge to marry them at five o'clock in the afternoon, after a workday for both of them.

Ria had gone home to bathe and change. This was a necessary rite, but it was still a wedding. Her wedding. She had hoped that dressing for it would make her feel better about it. It was too late to be having second thoughts, but now she questioned her decision to tell Taylor about the child.

After having been assured by her doctor that she was indeed pregnant, she had decided that she and the father would be married before the child was born. During that sleepless night, she had envisioned Taylor and her signing a document legally binding them, then signing another document legally severing them after the baby was born.

Things like sharing a house and the same last name hadn't figured in her mental pictures, any more than did the white-and-apricot rosebud bouquet he'd given her when he'd picked her up. The mandatory marriage had been humanized, but she couldn't put a finger on exactly when that had happened.

The bouquet trembled in her hands as she recited her vows before the judge and his secretary/witness. When the judge called for the ring, Taylor surprised her by taking a plain gold band from his vest pocket and sliding it on her finger.

And when the judge granted them permission to kiss, Taylor put all his expertise into it, convincing both smiling witnesses that this was a love match. The kiss almost convinced his breathless bride, and she knew better.

They left the courthouse as newlyweds. Ria, still

rattled over the solemnizing kiss, said, "You shouldn't have bothered with the ring."

"I make it a rule never to shortchange my wives," Taylor said, sending a dazzling smile down her way.

"I'm your first."

"I'm setting a precedent." He helped her into the Corvette. "I've made dinner reservations at La Fleur."

The groom was chock-full of surprises. "I wish you hadn't."

"Aren't you hungry?"

"Not very," she replied evasively.

"Are you feeling sick?"

She toyed with the idea of lying, but decided that that wasn't a very auspicious way to begin any marriage. "No, it's not that."

He wheeled the Vet beneath the porte cochere, but ignored the parking attendant who bounded up to the side of the car. "Then what is it, Ria?"

"It's everything. The bouquet, the ring, the dinner. It's all so . . . so bridal."

"You don't like roses? You wanted a silver ring? A diamond? La Fleur isn't your favorite restaurant?"

"Damn you, stop making jokes. You know what I'm trying to say."

"No, I don't. Why don't you spell it out for me?"

"All right, I will. Don't go overboard with this thing."

Agitated, he pulled his bottom lip through his teeth while he studied her. "I'm supposed to be crazy in love with you, aren't I? Enough to get married impulsively. Wouldn't you say a man in that shape is likely to go overboard?"

"You didn't marry me impulsively and you aren't crazy in love."

"But they don't know that," he hissed, indicating the world in general beyond the windshield. "We've got to make this convincing."

"So your political career won't be jeopardized?" she asked snidely.

His jaw muscles contracted and his eyes turned a frigid blue. Leaning forward, he enunciated, "No, so people won't find out that you screwed a total stranger and got knocked up on Christmas Eve."

All the color drained from Ria's face while, conversely, the sour contents of her stomach surged up the back of her throat. "I'm going to be sick." Frantically she groped for the door handle.

Tossing the car keys to the parking attendant, Taylor rushed her inside. She made it into the ladies' room just in time. Afterward, the elderly attendant commiserated and offered her cold compresses. She laid one against Ria's clammy forehead and the other against her throat.

"I've been telling that bartender he's mixing drinks too strong," the attendant said, patting Ria's hand.

"I haven't had anything to drink. I'm—" She started to say, "I'm pregnant," but amended it to, "I just got married."

The woman's creased face broke into a broad smile. "Wedding night jitters? You'll soon get over them."

Ria smiled weakly. When she was certain that the nausea had subsided, she applied fresh lipstick and left, the attendant's best wishes for a happy life ringing in her ears.

Taylor was pacing just outside the lounge. "Are you all right?"

"Better."

He looked almost as sick as she'd been. "Ria, I'm sorry. Lord, that was a terrible thing for me to say."

"Yes, it was. But I accept your apology, because I was being so bitchy." She was assailed by emotion, and her eyes filled with tears she was powerless to hold back. A search through her small bag failed to produce a Kleenex, but Taylor handed her a monogrammed handkerchief. "I provoked you," she said. "You've been so considerate. I expected you to be surly and difficult about all this. I was prepared for your scorn, but not your kindness." She raised her head and noticed that they had attracted a small audience. "Everyone's watching."

"Don't worry about it. Brides are expected to cry," he said, "especially when the groom takes off his pants." She was laughing when he took her elbow and led her into an alcove, where there were pay telephones and cigarette-vending machines. It afforded them some privacy.

"Ria." He rested his hand against her cheek. "What I said in the car . . . that was a very ugly word to use for something as miraculous as making a baby. And . . ."

"What?" she asked after his pause was extended.

"I never thought of what happened between us as just screwing."

Their long, telling stare was broken by a man who came in to use the telephone. "We don't have to stay if you don't feel well," Taylor said, blotting her cheeks with his handkerchief before repocketing it.

"Yes, please, I want to. You went to all the trouble of making the reservation. It would be a shame to waste it."

She could tell by his smile that he was pleased. The *maître d'* politely inquired if Ms. Lavender was all right. She assured him that she was, and Taylor told him, "It's Mrs. MacKensie now, Peter."

The head waiter, who knew both of them by name, admirably recovered from his surprise and said, "Congratulations, Mr. MacKensie."

He bowed formally to Ria, then showed them to the best table in the restaurant and sent over a complimentary bottle of champagne. Within minutes everyone in the kitchen, the staff of waiters, the other diners, even the parking valet, who was giving the Corvette an almost sexual rubdown, had heard that Mayor-elect MacKensie had married the architect Ria Lavender.

"Don't you get tired of men looking at you with unadulterated lust?"

She lowered the embossed leather folder that held her menu and gazed at him over the top of it. Her eyes were no longer vacuous, and color was coming back into her cheeks. "What did you say?"

"Every head in the place turned when you walked through."

"You imagined that."

"Uh-uh. A dozen pairs of covetous eyes stabbed me in the back. I feel sorry for the poor, deprived suckers, but that doesn't mean I'll stand for their ogling my wife." Ria knew he was talking foolishness only to make her feel better, but it was working. She even warmed under the lazy inspection his eyes gave her. "New dress?"

She hated to admit that she had bought the suit for the wedding ceremony, especially after having accused him of placing too much importance on it. The ecru linen two-piece suit had a slender skirt and a well-fitted one-button jacket with a single, wide lapel of matching cotton lace. A strand of pearls was nestled in the hint of cleavage that showed.

"Yes, it's new, but I didn't buy it just for today. I needed it anyway."

Taylor smiled teasingly. "The pearls, are they a gift from a man?"

"My parents. College graduation."

He nodded curtly and with satisfaction. "What do you feel like eating?"

"Campbell's chicken broth."

He snickered from behind his menu. "Then order the consommé. That's what you'll get."

Ria was surprised that she could eat an entire grilled chicken breast. For dessert the management sent out a complimentary frosted white cake only large enough for two. To the delight of the restaurant staff, Taylor sliced it ceremoniously. They fed each other bites and made toasts with champagne, though Ria barely sipped hers.

When it came time to leave, Taylor assisted her out of her chair and kept a solicitous hand on the small of her back as they headed for the exit. They had just reached the *maître d*'s desk when they came face-to-face with a trio waiting to be seated.

The unattached blonde's eyes drifted over Ria without really seeing her. She smiled radiantly at Taylor. "Taylor, how wonderful to run into you. You're not leaving, are you? It's so early. We just got here. You remember the Wilsons?"

"Of course," Taylor said, shaking hands with the man and nodding to his wife.

"Why don't you join us?" the blonde suggested. She included Ria in the invitation only by glancing in her general direction before turning her hungry eyes on Taylor.

"Sorry, not tonight. Ria, this is Lisa Burton. Lisa this is Ria, my wife."

The Wilsons saved the awkward moment from becoming a total fiasco. Both women were stunned speechless. Ria recovered faster than Lisa did. She acknowledged the introductions and responded to Mrs. Wilson's inquiry about whether she was the architect she'd heard so much about.

Lisa breached every rule of etiquette and cut straight to the heart of the matter as soon as she'd recovered her power of speech. "Isn't this rather sudden, Taylor?"

"This" didn't have to be clarified. Lisa's eyes were dark with malice. Taylor draped an arm across Ria's shoulders. "I met Ria last fall."

Late, late last fall, Ria thought.

"We got married this afternoon." Having divulged all the information he planned to, he nudged Ria forward. "Now, if you'll excuse us, we're in a hurry to get home."

Ria's knees were about to buckle and her cheeks were hot with embarrassment over Taylor's implication that the wedding night was about to commence. She was desperately glad to rush out of the restaurant on his arm. She held herself together by crossing her arms tightly over her midsection while they waited for the attendant to bring the car around. Taylor, humming off key, perused the lost-and-found and opportunities-for-employment notices tacked to a bulletin board on the garage wall.

Once she was seated in the Corvette, Ria rested her head in her hand. "You're not going to toss the consommé, are you?" he asked. " 'Cause if you are, I'd appreciate it if you'd give me time to pull over and stop."

"Taylor, I just met Lisa. Your Lisa. Did you see the expression on her face when you told her I was your wife? How can you be so blasé about it?"

"I don't want to talk about Lisa," he said tightly.

"Obviously, but I think we should."

Stubbornly he clenched his jaw and said nothing. They reached his house, but Ria barely glanced at her new home. She was too perturbed at Taylor for keeping her in suspense about his girlfriend. He came around to help her out and carried her suitcase up to the front door, which he unlocked. It swung open, but Ria refused to step inside.

"Waiting for me to carry you across the threshold?"

"I'm waiting for you to tell me about Lisa."

He dropped the suitcase and placed both his hands on the wall behind her, trapping her head between his arms. "Let's get this straight right now. She's not, nor ever has been, *my* Lisa. If having slept with her makes her mine, then she's also belonged to lots of other men. Got that? And I don't owe her any explanations. It was purely coincidental that I had a broken date with her on the night I met you." He lowered his hands. "Now, unless you want to have our second quarrel as a married couple out here on the front porch, I suggest you drop the subject of Lisa and let me carry you across the threshold."

She let him, because she didn't have any choice when he picked her up. But she couldn't forget the dumbfounded expression on that woman's face. The affair might have been just that to Taylor, but Lisa Burton had attached considerably more importance to it. However, for the time being, and for the sake of harmony, she let the subject drop.

Taylor carried her not only inside, but through the entire house. "This is the kitchen." Everything in it was stark white, with the exception of the walls, which were terra cotta. "It's got all the modern conveniences."

"Will you please put me down?"

"No."

"But I can't explore."

"A euphemism for meddle, and there'll be plenty of time for that later. You need to get off your feet. I think your ankles are beginning to swell."

"They are?"

Panicked, Ria raised one foot and examined her ankle. It was as trim as ever. She glared up at Taylor. He burst out laughing. "Gotcha."

Ria felt his laughter vibrating through her breasts, and it was contagious. They exchanged farcical comments about the living room, the casual den, and all the other rooms in the house. But her laughter ceased the moment he opened the door to the master bedroom.

A wall of windows opened onto a sweeping mountain vista. The recent sunset had left the sky a vivid purple backdrop for a crescent moon and Venus in all its glory.

One glance at the spacious room and Ria knew she had married a sybarite. The carpet was ankle deep. There was a king-sized platform bed dressed up in a black leather bed sack. At the foot of the bed lay a mink throw rug that looked downright iniquitous. The lighting was subtle, multi-directional, and seemingly without source. A black marble fireplace was built into the wall opposite the bed. Low chairs invited one to curl up and enjoy what the high-tech entertainment center had to offer. A crystal bowl of white tulips decorated the bedside table. On the other side of the bed, a bottle of champagne was chilling in a silver cooler.

As an architect, Ria could appreciate the room's exquisite design. As a woman, it made her tremble like a virgin looking into the pirate captain's cabin.

Taylor released her, letting her down slowly and keeping his hands on her shoulders as though she might bolt.

"Very nice," Ria said lightly. "Wonder what the citizens of our fair city would think of their mayor-elect if they could see these hedonistic sleeping quarters?"

His chuckle was rich and deep and stirring against her ear. His hands were moving up and down her arms. "They'd probably like me better."

"They probably would. Especially the women."

"Then you like it?"

She faced him. "It really doesn't matter, since I won't be sleeping in here."

Crossing his arms and his ankles, he propped himself against the doorjamb. "Ria, when I talked you into living with me for the duration of our marriage, I might have forgotten to mention one tiny detail."

Her tummy went weightless, knowing what was coming. "What?"

"This is a large house, but it only has one bedroom."

"Fine. I'll sleep on the couch."

"Not on my couch, you won't. I wouldn't hear of letting my pregnant wife sleep on a couch."

Ria raised her chin a notch. "You browbeat me into agreeing that we should live together to make this marriage look on the level. But it was our understanding that we wouldn't be sleeping together."

"That was your understanding," he said in a disturbingly quiet voice.

She squared her shoulders. "Before I stay here, some kind of sleeping arrangements must be made."

"They've already been made." He moved away from the door and reached behind him to close it. "I take the left side of the bed."

Four

"You aren't serious." For an answer Taylor removed his suit coat and tossed it into the nearest pillow-laden chair. Ria stared at him with dismay. "I can't believe this. Do you intend to use force?"

He merely frowned.

"That's the only way you'll get me into bed with you."

"Now, Ria, don't go saying words you'll have to eat." His grin would have bared fangs if he'd had them.

He had already taken off his vest and was working on the buttons of his shirt. Ria nervously moistened her lips, trying not to notice how dextrous his strong, lean fingers were.

When all the buttons were undone, he slowly pulled the shirttail from his waistband. The Chippendale men could take lessons from him on how to disrobe alluringly. The shirt parted to reveal a muscled chest covered by a blanket of dark curly hair that Ria remembered all too well. That impressive chest had played vital roles in recent fantasies.

"Look, Taylor," she said quickly when he dropped the shirt and lowered his hands to his belt, "what happened on Christmas Eve—"

"Was fantastic. Why pretend it wasn't? And why not enjoy it again?"

"Because it didn't mean anything."

"So?"

"That's . . . that's animalistic."

"Riiiiight." He only laughed at her exasperation. "A healthy case of lust is good for the body, mind, and soul."

"I don't think so. Look what happened to me the last time I indulged it."

No longer smiling, he demanded, "Don't you think the baby is significant?"

She sucked in her breath sharply. "Yes. If I hadn't, I would have gotten rid of it as soon as I suspected I was pregnant."

"The baby, if nothing else, makes what happened on Christmas Eve special." His expression softened. "I'm a man and you're a woman, and you can deny it till Doomsday, Ria, but we're physically attracted to each other. There doesn't need to be any more justification than that for us to make love."

He stepped forward; she took a cautious step backward.

"When in doubt, the laws of Nature prevail," he said. "Just like on Christmas Eve. It would be stupid for us to live under the same roof, liking each other, even a little, wanting each other, I believe a lot, and not take advantage of the situation."

"But it's temporary."

"That makes it even better. We're not under any pressure to make the marriage work, only to enjoy its fringe benefits."

She'd run out of space for her retreat. The bed,

with its leather and fur enticements, was catching the backs of her knees.

"We know exactly where we stand with each other," he went on. "Most couples who get married aren't that lucky."

"You can rationalize anything."

"Then consider it from a practical point of view. This is my wedding night. I want to spend it like a groom. As a bride, don't you feel entitled to some recreational sex?" He drew her against him and ducked his head to nuzzle her exposed throat. "We can continue arguing if you want to, but in the long run"—he nibbled his way up the cord of her neck, then positioned his mouth directly above hers—"you'll lose."

His hard, long, hungry kiss left her weak and needy. She wrapped her arms around his neck for support, and for gratification curved her body against the front of his.

"Hm, that feels good." Cupping her hips, he pulled her tighter against him. He took the combs from her hair and buried his nose in the waves tumbling over his face.

Unfastening the single button on the jacket of her suit, he slipped his hands inside and covered her breasts. He was sensitive enough to feel her initial, shrinking reaction.

"Tender?" he whispered. She nodded. He opened the jacket and gazed at her full breasts, filling and spilling over the lace cups of her demi-bra. He kissed the rounded top curves gently, then reluctantly raised his head.

"No, it's okay," she said quickly.

Deep in his throat he made a yearning sound. His lips made impressions in the soft, giving flesh. Moving his head to one side, he kissed her nipple through the lace. "Ria, say it was good."

"Christmas Eve? Yes, it was good."

"Sometimes I thought I'd dreamed it."

"I carry proof that you didn't."

"Yes, you do." He moved his hands down to her abdomen, covering it protectively. Then, holding her stare, his smile changed into an expression of intense desire. Seductively, he ground the heels of his hands against her mound and let his fingers conform to the tapering shape of her body. "I want you again. Now."

Speechlessly, breathlessly, Ria nodded.

There were whispers in the dark from seeking lips and from naked skin against leather, against mink, against lemon-scented sheets.

"No, leave the pearls on."

"But that looks positively wicked."

"It sure as hell does."

Soft laughter.

"You're beautiful, Ria. Very."

"So are you."

"Me? I'm all hairy."

"Uh-huh."

"You're all smooth and silky. I didn't take nearly enough time looking at you on Christmas Eve."

"You got around to touching everything, though."

"I intend to tonight too."

"Hm, Taylor."

"Is that uncomfortable?"

"No."

"Sure?"

"Yes."

"Do you like it?" Silence. "Ria?"

"Yes, yes, I like it."

"If I suck them, will it hurt?"

"No."

A soft hiss of pleasure. "You're so sweet."

"Don't stop, Taylor."

"I won't."

"And don't wait, either."

"I thought—"

"Please."

And much later champagne was poured over her body. It funneled from her belly into the V of her thighs. Its icy bubbles glistened in the tight, glossy curls before warm lips sipped them up one by one.

After that, when he asked her, "More champagne?" her entire body blushed. He laughed. "I'll drink it from a glass this time."

"I wasn't complaining about the last time."

He muttered a curse, bent over her, cupped her face between his hands, and kissed her fervently. "That was my special way of toasting my bride." He kissed her again. "God, you're gorgeous."

She declined the champagne, having sworn off alcohol because of the child she carried. But he poured himself a glass and, leaning against the pillows unselfconsciously naked and semiaroused, lazily and possessively gazed at her.

"We should have a very attractive kid," he said.

"Dark hair, for sure."

"And tall."

She ran her hand up his thigh. "Nice long legs."

"Nice long . . . never mind."

"That too"—she giggled—"if it's a boy."

Grabbing a handful of her hair, Taylor drew her head up for another scorching kiss. When they fell apart he said, "I wonder if he'll be a he."

"Do you think it's a girl?"

He shrugged. "It won't matter to me."

"Me either." She ran her hand over her stomach and said reflectively, "I just want him to be healthy and happy."

"He will be," Taylor gently assured her. "Will he have blue eyes or green? Which are dominant?" Ria said nothing. Taylor rubbed her cheeks with the backs of his fingers and traced the frown that had formed between her brows. "What?"

Sighing, she rested her cheek against his thigh. "I was just thinking that we don't know what kind of genes he or she will inherit from my parents. My real parents."

"To have produced you, they must have been ideal physical specimens of superior intelligence. At least one of them had a stubborn streak and a short temper." He playfully tugged on a strand of ebony hair. "My guess is that you have some Indian heritage, with your hair and cheekbones." He traced the high cheekbone with the tip of his index finger.

"No doubt. I used to daydream about them." She had never confided in anyone about her parents, and wondered why she found it so easy to talk about them to Taylor. "In my fantasies, my mother was an Indian princess and my father an Irish adventurer with fierce green eyes. But the parents I imagined were reminiscent of characters I had read about in historical romance novels, not contemporary people. And I imagined that there was a disaster that took their lives and made me an orphan."

"How do you know that didn't happen?"

"Mom and Dad told me that my parents were alive; at least they were at the time I was adopted."

He ran his hand over her head and down her back. "Who named you Ria?"

"Mom and Dad."

"Have you told them about the baby?"

There was a brief pause before she said, "No."

"About me?"

Coming to a sitting position, she said, "Forgive me, Taylor, but yes, I did. I told them that I'd met someone and that it was very likely we'd be getting married."

"What was their reaction?"

"They were excited about the prospect of a son-in-law. I think they were afraid I was a dyed-in-the-wool feminist career woman who scoffed at marriage, hearth, and home."

"They weren't too far off."

She made a face at him. "Mom wanted to start planning parties and organizing a large church wedding. I forestalled her by saying that you were a public official and wanted to get married with as little fanfare as possible. I hated lying to them, but— "

"But this way we can let them know we're married, yet wait and set our anniversary in accordance with the baby's birthday."

She stared down at her hands. "Why hurt them needlessly?"

He tipped her chin up. "Exactly."

"Thank you, Taylor."

He set his empty champagne glass on the nightstand and kissed her. "It's late, and tomorrow is a workday."

"Yes, we'd better get some sleep."

"Like hell," he said with a growl, lifting her to straddle his lap. "We'd better get on to phase two."

"Hi."

"Hi."

"How was your day?"

"Fine. Yours?"

"Fine."

Awkwardly they faced each other. Taylor had just come home and found Ria in the kitchen. He still had his briefcase in his hand. She was wearing an apron and holding a long-handled spoon.

They had overslept that morning. In their rush to get to work, there hadn't been time for them to be embarrassed over their night together. They had taken quick showers. Ria had panicked when she upended her suitcase and discovered that half of what she needed to get dressed had been left at home—at her home. Taylor's favorite necktie had been misplaced and couldn't be found. Ria burned her finger on her curling iron. After drinking a cup of tepid instant coffee made with tap water, Taylor had raced out the back door, shouting over his shoulder that he would see her later.

Now it was later. They were standing face-to-face, under no pressing deadline, and each was curious yet hesitant to know the other's opinion of their first twenty-four hours as Mr. and Mrs. MacKensie.

"Something smells good," he said, setting his briefcase on the kitchen table.

"Pot roast."

"I thought we'd go out."

"You don't like pot roast?" Ria asked anxiously.

"I love pot roast," he rushed to say. "I just don't want you to think you have to cook every night."

"I don't." She waved her hand negligently and pushed back a strand of hair. "I wanted to make up for breakfast this morning. Or the lack thereof."

"I don't eat breakfast anyway."

"You don't? Oh, well, good. Neither do I. Especially these days." She laid a hand on her tummy. "But you left for work without having any morning coffee. That's cruel and unusual punishment."

He forced a smile at her forced joke. "How long before dinner?"

"Half an hour."

"I've got time for a shower, then?"

"Yes. Don't rush. Dinner will keep until we're ready for it."

"Okay." He picked up his briefcase again and headed for the door. But there he paused, his back still to her. Slowly he turned around. "Ria?"

Her head snapped up. "What?"

The briefcase hit the floor. In no longer than it took for him to lunge across the kitchen, Ria was in his arms and they were kissing madly. Ria threw her arms around his neck. The spoon dripped gravy down his back, but neither of them noticed or cared. He pulled her up hard and high against the front of his body. They were laughing and struggling for air by the time they broke apart.

"Then you're not sorry you married me?" she asked. "Now that you've had time to think about it for one whole day?"

"Are you kidding? I haven't come home to pot roast since my mother died."

"Is that the only reason you're glad?"

He rubbed his middle against hers. "Stupid question, Ria." They kissed again. "Let's start over. How was your day?"

"I took off early, then went by the house and packed my car with another load."

"I should paddle you for that. You didn't carry anything in, did you?"

"No. By that time I was exhausted."

"You shouldn't have bothered to cook dinner."

"I rested first. Oh, maybe I should warn you that I'm having a van deliver all my plants here tomorrow."

"We might have to move out. There won't be room for all of us."

Smiling happily, she asked, "How was your day?"

"In a word, a bitch."

"That's two words."

"I've married a smart-ass, hey?" Grasping that particular part of her anatomy, he bent his head and gnawed at her neck until she begged for mercy. "We had a closed-door city council meeting today. There was a row about a pending tax hike. At the office, a set of specifications had been lost and

the client raised hell with us until they were found."
He planted a soft kiss on the tip of her nose. "And
in the midst of all that chaos, all I could think
about was that soft little hiccupping sound you
make when you come."

"Taylor!"

"Taylor!" he mimicked. "If you don't want me to
think about it, then stop making the sound."

"Or stop coming."

He said with a snarl, "I dare you not to."

One kiss led to another, until more than the
oven was warming up the kitchen. Finally Ria
pushed him away. "Go take your shower. I'll have
a drink waiting for you when you get out."

Over dinner they discussed their new marital
status and what ramifications it would have on
their lives. "Did you tell the people at work?" he
asked her.

"Yes. They were all surprised."

"All but Guy."

Taylor's indifference didn't fool Ria. He was as
curious about Guy and his reaction to their marriage as she was about Lisa Burton's. "I guess it's
no longer a secret to him whose baby I'm carrying."

"If he has any doubts on that subject, send him
to me."

She enjoyed Taylor's jealousy, even if it was more
for the baby than for her.

"Prepare yourself to get a few phone calls tomorrow," he said as he helped himself to more pot
roast. "My secretary is delivering a press release
to the newspaper and radio stations in the morning, announcing my marriage to Ms. Ria Lavender."

Ria set down her fork and looked at him wor-
riedly. "I hope this doesn't jeopardize your being
sworn in as mayor."

"I won the election fair and square."

"I know, but there might be some eyebrows
raised."

"I think everyone who voted for me will be pleased and proud about their choice. They'll be relieved that I'm no longer a swinging single, which, as you know, was a campaign issue. Our marriage justifies the confidence they placed in me." Ria had picked up her fork again, but was only shifting the food from one side of her plate to the other. "Okay, spill it."

She met his eyes levelly. "In your office that day, you accused me of wanting to ruin your career. I hope that doesn't happen after all."

He reached for her hand. "It won't."

"When they find out about the baby—"

"Everyone will be delighted. The whole city will probably make a big fuss over him. He'll be the most celebrated kid ever to hit town." He stroked the back of her hand with his thumb. "And about that accusation, I didn't mean it. I was still trying to pick myself up and dust myself off."

"You didn't believe me when I first told you that the baby was yours."

"Yes, I did."

"You did?"

"Right away."

"Why?"

"Any woman who would worry about besting someone in a battle over a shrimp would never lie about something as important as a baby." He lifted her palm to his mouth and kissed it. "Go rest. I'll clean up."

"That doesn't look like resting to me," he told her half an hour later, when he went into the den and found her leaning over a drawing board. Between his shower and dinner he had moved her things from the car, depositing clothes and shoes in the massive closet in the bedroom and setting up her drawing board in this room, as she'd asked him to.

"Doesn't that hurt your back?"

She smiled at him over her shoulder, but returned her attention to the design she had been sketching out. "I'm used to it." He came up behind her and propped his chin on her shoulder. "What do you think?" she asked.

"It doesn't look much like me," he said, tilting his head and staring at the drawing dubiously.

"You nut." She bumped her bottom against him, and he grunted with pleasure.

"What is it?"

"It's my house. See, here's the front door and the living room. I'm trying to decide where to build on a nursery. Should I go up or out?" He said nothing. "Taylor?"

"Don't you like it here?" he asked in a low voice.

"Of course. This is a beautiful house. But I've got to have the remodeling done on my own before the baby is born, so we'll have a place to live."

"Oh."

His body was curved around hers, so she felt the tension of dislike in every hard muscle. Did he hate the thought of her leaving or of having to make appointments with her to see his child? Diplomatically she scooted that set of plans aside and unrolled another blueprint, effectively changing the subject. They had seven months to work out a dual-custody agreement.

"What's that?" Taylor asked.

"Patio homes, which is a fancy term for duplexes. My client is building three sets."

"Speaking of sets." He reached around her and scooped her breasts into his palms. "Did you go braless to the office?"

"Certainly not."

"So you only took it off when you got home, to drive your husband to distraction?"

Ria held back the sigh that filled her throat.

Ripples of sensation were eddying out from the circular massage of his hands and spreading down through her feminity. "No," she said unsteadily. "I left it off because it's binding. All my bras are too small now, and I haven't had time to replace them."

"Don't rush out and buy larger ones on my account." Moving her ponytail aside with his chin, he kissed her behind the ear. His thumbs gently fanned the tips of her breasts. "Our kid is gonna be so lucky." Sliding his hands beneath her top, he simulated sucking motions with his fingers.

"Taylor, what are you doing?"

"In the vernacular, feeling you up. Scientifically it's called breast-feeding preparedness. Whatever, it's producing the desired results."

He was hard and full against her bottom. Ria's head dropped forward. Her elbows supported her against the drawing board. "I took off early today," she said breathily. "I've got work to catch up on." Her protests sounded halfhearted at best.

"Go on with what you were doing. Don't mind me." He moved one hand down to the snap of her jeans and undid it. The zipper came next.

"But I can't concentrate when you're doing that." She moaned as he slid his hand into her panties.

"I don't think you were concentrating solely on your work," he chided softly.

She heard the smile in his voice and knew that her body had betrayed her. She sighed his name. The mastery of his thumb was breathtaking. "Hm, Taylor, what's the scientific name for this?"

"Foreplay."

Ria was suspicious of the ease with which they settled into married life. She braced herself for the day when Taylor would come home cranky after work. It never happened. She braced herself for the morning he'd wake up in a bad mood. That never happened either. She expected to uncover some carefully concealed flaw in his personality. It remained concealed.

If he arrived home before she did, he was waiting when she came in, with a cool drink, a pillow for her back, and a foot rub. They ate out more than she cooked, though she told him repeatedly that she didn't mind cooking.

He took her to the offices of MacKensie Electrical Contractors, Inc., and introduced her to all his employees. On the way home he teased her about throwing some business their way. They had often remarked on how strange it was that, given their professions, they'd never worked on the same projects. It seemed that destiny had brought them together for a purpose on Christmas Eve. Ria liked to think that purpose was the child she carried.

Taylor picked her up for lunch one day at Bishop and Harvey. He and Guy Patterson shook hands, but there was a distinct chill in the air when they were introduced. Taylor was especially attentive and ardent in bed that night.

As the date for his official swearing-in as mayor approached, he was frequently called upon to serve as an after-dinner speaker at clubs and civic organizations. Ria always attended these affairs with him, smiling for photographers, shaking hands, meeting people on Taylor's behalf.

On the drive home after one such function, Taylor reached across the car and laid a hand on her knee. "I know all this is boring for you. You're a real trouper. I appreciate your attitude very much. Thanks."

She started to tell him that she was never bored when watching and listening to him. But she refrained. Endearments were only exchanged in bed at the height of passion. If she was tempted to express her growing affection for him, she reminded herself that their marriage was temporary and that it would be better in the long run to keep her feelings to herself.

They listened to each other's ideas, laughed at each other's jokes, shared past heartaches. They made love. Frequently.

But what was most surprising to Ria was Taylor's profound interest in the baby. During the first two weeks of their marriage, he became a prenatal expert, buying every book available on the subject. He hounded her with questions.

When will it start moving?

When will we be able to listen to its heartbeat?

Can you feel it?

Do women really carry boys differently than girls?

Most of the sentences began with a question word and had something to do with the baby. One night he joined her in bed, where she was glancing over her agenda for the coming week. He began reading aloud from the text of a picture book on fetal life.

"Isn't that amazing?" he asked, marveling over a fact he'd just discovered. Cupping his hands over her stomach, he shouted, "Hello in there. Do you really already have a thumbprint?"

Ria gave his shoulder a shove. "He's got a mentally unbalanced father. I know that for fact." He untied the belt of her robe. "Stop that," Ria cried, laughing and swatting away his hands.

"I've got to check you out."

"Check me out?"

"To make sure you're doing everything right."

"I went to the doctor yesterday. He checked me out and charged a very handsome fee for doing it."

"But I'm going according to the book." He raised the book and shook it as though it were Holy Writ in the hands of a prophet. "And I don't charge near as much as the doctor."

Laughing at his adorable insanity, Ria let him open her robe. She was naked underneath. Consulting the open book, Taylor muttered, "Let's see now, page one. Are your breasts noticeably larger?" He tested one by kneading it gently. "I'd say so. Up one millimeter from last week."

Ria rolled her eyes. "Should we document this?"

"Hush, I'm concentrating. Page two." He turned one of the wide, glossy pages. "Ah-ha! Are your nipples changing color?" He brushed his fingers across her nipples. They responded. "Hm. Slightly. I think the kid will know what to do with them."

But just in case he didn't, Taylor showed him.

As his soft, wet mouth caressed her, Ria began to move restlessly beneath him. She arched her back, pushing her breast deeper into his mouth. She ran her fingers through his dark hair and held his head against her.

He swept his hand down her lower body. "Rounded abdomen. Taut. Good, good," he said, panting against her skin. "Perfect. Perfect mother. Perfect wife. Perfect woman."

Five

"Ria?"

She glanced up from her desk. Guy Patterson was standing in the doorway of her office. She'd seen little of him since she had told the firm's associates of her marriage. He had avoided her. She didn't blame him. It was well known that they'd been going out together for quite some time. For her suddenly to marry another man, especially one as dynamic as Taylor MacKensie, must have made Guy lose face. She hoped they could still be friends, but his dour expression didn't hold much promise of that.

"Hello, Guy. Come in."

"Actually I was sent to fetch you. The partners have called an emergency meeting."

She rose from her chair. "What's up?"

"I think I'd better let them tell you." He stood aside and let her precede him, pointedly ignoring the question in her eyes. Together and in silence, they walked down the carpeted hallway and into the serene boardroom, where the executives of Bishop and Harvey were already congregated.

The atmosphere was unnaturally subdued as they took their places around the massive walnut table. Ria thought that either she was becoming paranoid or everyone was indeed treating her to covert glances.

"Thank you for coming on such short notice. I know you're busy, but this matter concerns all of us, and it's highly important." Mr. Bishop, the founder of the firm, had retired three years earlier. Mr. Harvey, his nephew, served as president and presided at all the meetings.

"Being awarded the contract for the Community Arts Center would mean a great deal to the firm," he began. "I'm sure you're aware of that."

The city's proposed arts complex had been under consideration for years. A bond issue had been passed in the previous year's election. That funding, along with private donations, was now making it possible for plans to come to fruition. The city had begun taking bids on various aspects of the Center's construction. Bishop and Harvey was one of the architectural firms being considered. It would be a massive, prestigious, highly profitable project.

"The city council is in the process of reviewing and eliminating bids," Mr. Harvey went on to say. "We hope that when all the others have been eliminated, we'll still be a strong contender for the contract. However . . ." He halted, coughed. Several others around the table shifted uncomfortably in their chairs. As a body, they were like an ailing animal, restless and malcontent.

Ria felt that it was time to put them out of their misery. "Does this impromptu meeting have anything to do with my recent marriage to Councilman and Mayor-elect MacKensie, Mr. Harvey?"

He couldn't have looked at her more gratefully if she'd thrown him a lifeline in a turbulent ocean.

"Everyone here is delighted about your marriage," he said, including that "everyone" in his happy grin. When his eyes lighted on Guy Patterson, he coughed unnecessarily again and blustered on. "But the public might see this as . . . What I mean to say is . . . The firm wouldn't want to lose the contract because of a conflict of interest."

"My husband and I haven't even discussed the Community Arts Center."

"I'm sure two newlyweds have had other things to talk about." A polite twitter of laughter circulated around the table. Mr. Harvey looked pleased with his troops, then turned serious when he faced Ria. "We must guard against anything that smacks of kickbacks or favors."

Ria pressed a hand against her chest. "There's been no such thing! Are you accusing me of—"

The president of Bishop and Harvey held up both hands. "Good Lord, no, Ms. Lavender, uh, Mrs. MacKensie. I'm not impugning your integrity or your husband's. You can see, however, what a dilemma this could turn into and how delicate the balance is. Millions of dollars are involved. If we're granted the contract, a rival might jump to the wrong conclusion as to why."

"Well, that would be their problem, wouldn't it? This firm had bid on the contract before I even met Mr. MacKensie. Surely—" Ria fell silent.

One passing glance at the faces of the people around the table told her that her protests were falling on unsympathetic ears. Everyone in the company liked her personally and admired her work. She'd made a contribution to the firm and had proved her worth several times over.

But getting the Community Arts Center contract would mean money in their pockets. Lots of it. Being denied the contract, for any reason, would cost them not only money, but prestige.

"Mr. Harvey," Ria said softly, "may I see you alone in your office, please?"

Once her decision had been made, she was in a hurry to get home and tell Taylor. She had tried to track him down by telephone, but couldn't reach him at either office. She felt good about her decision and was anxious to share it with him and gauge his reaction.

He was making a pitcher of wine coolers when she entered the living room at a near run and tossed her briefcase into the nearest chair.

"Taylor, I need to talk to you."

"What happened to hello?"

"Hello."

"Hi. I didn't hear your car. How was your day?"

"Up and down."

"I'm sorry."

"No, it came out okay. Will you sit down, please?"

"Well, I'm kinda busy, and—"

"This won't take long."

"I hope not, because there's—"

"Please, Taylor, listen to me. I've thought this through, and—" The doorbell cut her off. "Are you expecting someone?"

"That's what I've been trying to work in edge-wise," Taylor told her as he crossed the room. He opened the door and invited an attractive woman inside. "Ria, this is Delia Starr, a reporter for the *Telegram*. She wants to do an article on us for this Sunday's edition."

"Uh, hello." Ria recovered enough to shake hands with the reporter.

"Let's all sit down." Taylor was looking strangely at Ria.

"Will you please excuse me? Ms. Starr, Delia, I got in from work just seconds before you arrived,"

Ria explained, knowing she looked harried. "I'd like to freshen up."

"I understand," the woman said. "Take your time. I have plenty of questions to ask Mayor-elect MacKensie. Maybe I should warn you that a photographer is joining me later to take pictures."

Ria rushed into the bedroom and closed the door. "Damn." She had been psyched up to tell Taylor what she'd done, and now it would have to wait.

In the bathroom/dressing room, she repaired her makeup, brushed her hair, and changed into slacks and a blouse. The outfit looked softer and more feminine than her business suit. She had noted that Taylor had changed from his suit into a more "at home with the MacKensies" look.

Fortifying herself with a deep breath, she rejoined them in the living room. Taylor stopped talking the moment she came in. He stood, took both her hands, and led her to the short, soft sofa where he was sitting. Handing her a club soda and lime, he peered inquiringly at her. Her reassuring smile told him that everything was okay.

"Did I miss anything?" she asked brightly.

"Just boring background stuff about my interest in local politics," he said.

"I don't think anything about your husband is boring," Delia Starr told Ria.

"Neither do I." Taylor had aroused, amused, and angered her, but he'd never bored her.

Ms. Starr asked Ria about her career as an architect, taking copious notes. Ria wondered if she noticed that Taylor was listening carefully too. Most of what Ria talked about he'd never heard before either.

"It's really uncanny that you picked today to interview us, Ms. Starr." Ria clasped her hands together nervously. "Because today marks a milestone in my career. I resigned from Bishop and Harvey."

"What?" Taylor looked at her mouth, as though lipreading, not trusting his ears to have heard her correctly. "You resigned?"

"Yes."

"Does your resignation have anything to do with the Community Arts Center project, Mrs. Mac-Kensie?"

"What about it?" Taylor demanded.

Ria placed a restraining hand on his arm. "Indirectly."

"Did they call for your resignation?" the reporter asked.

"No, Mr. Harvey was a perfect gentleman, as always. He said that he sincerely regretted losing me."

"But better you than a multimillion-dollar contract."

Ria ignored that well-placed shot. "Actually, the Community Arts Center controversy spurred me to do something that I've been thinking about doing for a long time."

"Quitting?" Delia asked.

"Resigning from Bishop and Harvey in order to set up my own firm."

Delia Starr was bent over her tablet, scribbling frantically. Ria looked at Taylor, surreptitiously shaking her head, warning him not to say anything until she'd had a chance to explain. "Taylor endorsed the idea wholeheartedly."

"Wholeheartedly," he echoed.

But the reporter was a veteran, and not that easily duped. "You seem surprised, Mr. MacKensie."

Taylor smiled at her engagingly. "I didn't know that Ria had reached her final decision. Congratulations, darling." He kissed her.

His kiss was tender and meaningful, but Ria

wondered if it were all for show. How did he really feel about her decision?

"Well, you can no longer be accused of conflict of interest," Delia said.

"No one had accused us of that." Taylor was still smiling, but his voice was steely. "For clarity's sake I think you should make a point of that in your story."

Delia Starr stared him down. "Why did you rush into marriage?"

The question was seemingly spontaneous and out of context, but both Ria and Taylor were savvy enough to recognize the bloodthirsty smile of a media shark.

Taylor, more accustomed to dealing with the press, responded easily. "It was a case of lust and love at first sight when we met. I don't believe in long engagements. I've been a bachelor for thirty-five years. When I saw Ria I knew why I'd stayed single. I'd been waiting for her."

He gazed down at his wife and squeezed her hand.

"It wasn't a shotgun wedding?"

Reflexively Taylor's grip tightened around Ria's hand. She held her breath. The reporter was making notes again. Finally she looked up at them inquisitively.

"What a quaint term." Taylor's smile was narrow and cold. "Apparently you know that Ria is pregnant."

"Rumor would have it," she said. "Just so you don't waste our time by denying it, I spoke with some of Ria's associates at work."

Not some. One. Guy Patterson, Ria thought. He was the only one who knew about the baby.

"Yes, we're having a baby," Taylor said, placing his arm around Ria's shoulders and pulling her close. "And we're delighted."

"Come now, Councilman. You've just been elected mayor. Did your hasty marriage to Mrs. MacKensie have anything to do with the fact that she's pregnant with your child and that your constituents might frown on that kind of behavior from a public official?"

"I don't want to see anything in print that even hints at that."

"Because it might be damaging to your career?"

"No, because it might be damaging to yours." Taylor's voice was barely above a whisper, but it was potent with unspoken threats. "If you write a single slanderous word about Ria, I'll sue you and your newspaper for every cent you've got."

Ria focused on the reporter's impatiently tapping pencil. The tempo was almost hypnotic. "I married Taylor because I love him." The pencil ceased its tapping. From the corner of her eye, Ria saw Taylor look down at her with astonishment. For a moment they all sat as though petrified. Ria broke the silence by saying, "Delia, your glass is empty. Would you like another drink?"

"Why'd you say that?"

"What?" Ria asked nonchalantly. The Corvette's windows were rolled down. She was enjoying the feel of an early-spring wind blowing against her face and through her hair.

"Why'd you tell her that our marriage was a love match?"

Ria looked at her husband. "To save you from a fire-breathing dragon named Delia. Or vice versa. You looked ready to throttle her."

"I was."

"I couldn't let that happen. Ms. Starr would have loved writing down every abusive quote and printing each one in the Sunday paper. I shudder to think of the expletives she'd have had to delete. You've got me to thank for saving your image, Mayor MacKensie."

"Feeling smug, are you?"

"Shouldn't I be?"

He turned into a city park. They had decided to take out their cheeseburgers rather than suffer the invasion of a little-league baseball team in the fast-food restaurant.

"Yep, you should. In fact, you should be congratulated for your diplomacy. 'Delia, your glass is empty.' That pencil-wielding bitch was eating out of your hand by the time she left." He cut the motor and gave Ria a sidelong glance. "Not to mention that hot-for-your-bod photographer."

"I don't know what you mean." Ria opened her door and stepped out, taking the packaged food with her.

"Like hell." Taylor slammed his car door. " 'Your cheekbones were made for a camera, Ria, love.' "

"That's not what he said. He said, 'Your *high* cheekbones were made for a camera, Ria, love.' "

"Oh, forgive me," Taylor said wryly. "Which one's mine?"

"Double cheese? Here," she said, passing him the cheeseburger.

"Why didn't you get double cheese? I don't want a scrawny kid."

"You won't get one. I promise. Baby and I will blossom one of these days soon. We'll eat you out of house and home. In the meantime the doctor said it's normal to drop a few pounds."

He gave her a critical once-over. "You're too skinny."

"The photographer seemed to think I was plump in all the right places," she said, winking saucily.

Taylor threw a french fry at her. "You didn't fall for all that smooth talk, did you?"

"I thought he was sincere." She batted her eyes innocently.

Taylor shook his head. "He was hitting on you."

"You recognize the moves, I guess."

"Modesty prevents me from bragging," he said, grinning arrogantly. Then he frowned. "He was a strutting peacock with an old line, and his jeans were too tight."

"You wear yours just as tight."

"You noticed?" he asked, holding a french fry poised and ready to be devoured.

"I noticed."

"You like?"

"I like," she confessed softly.

His strong white teeth bit cleanly into the french fry. It reminded Ria of that fortuitous bite of Christmas turkey he had eaten from her fingers. She had to swallow hard to get her bite of cheeseburger down.

"What about you and Delia?" she asked as she munched. "She got awfully sweet after the two of you met on a plane of mutual antagonism. You were real chummy-chummy by the time she left. What was so interesting out by the mailbox when you walked her to her car? It certainly took a long time to say thank you and good-bye."

"Oh, that. Well, I thought, give the broad a break and let her ask one personal question."

"Did she?"

"Yes. She asked me if we engaged in oral sex."

Ria sputtered vanilla milk shake all over her face and his. "Taylor!"

Laughing, he wiped her face clean with a paper napkin.

Ria stared into her shake as she stirred it with the plastic straw. Her cheeks were pink, and it wasn't from being wind-chapped by riding with the windows down.

They finished eating. He was stuffing their trash into the sack when he said, "Back to my original question: Why'd you tell her that we'd married for love?"

"I didn't tell her that we had. I told her that I had."

"You're evading the question."

"I had to say something to blunt her fangs," she cried. "That seemed the most expedient thing to say. It worked, didn't it?"

"And that's the only reason you said it?"

"Of course." She couldn't look directly at him.

"It just kinda rolled off your tongue, spur-of-the-moment-like, huh?"

"Yes."

"It didn't have any basis in truth whatsoever?"

"None. If we had loved each other, it wouldn't have taken the baby to bring us back together, would it?"

Evening had fallen. The dusk was quiet and still. They didn't realize how quiet and still until they shared that long, silent stare.

Finally Taylor said, "I didn't call you because I knew you were already involved."

"I didn't ask."

"But I wanted to tell you." He yanked a new leaf off the nearest tree and shredded it. "You didn't call me either."

"I haven't made a habit of calling men for dates. That's another of my old-fashioned idiosyncrasies."

"It's perfectly acceptable these days for the woman to make the first move."

"It's not perfectly acceptable to me. That kind of aggressiveness seems masculine."

"You couldn't be masculine no matter how hard you tried."

"Well, even if I had wanted to call you, I wouldn't have."

"Why?"

"Your involvement with Lisa. You hardly made a secret of it on Christmas Eve. In fact, you told me more than I wanted to know." Ria raised her voice in spite of her best intentions to keep this discussion from becoming an argument.

"Why does Lisa always enter into it?"

"Because the only reason you were alone at the Grahams' was that she was out of town. Obviously the two of you were in the midst of a hot and heavy affair."

He thrust his face close to hers. "That didn't stop you from sleeping with me, did it?"

She recoiled, then attacked. Taylor was spoiling for a fight, and he was going to get one. "And sleeping with me didn't keep you from sneaking out the next morning."

"I didn't sneak."

"Ha!" She flung back her windblown hair. "I woke up to find you tiptoeing across my living-room floor, half your clothes and your shoes in hand. Doesn't that sound like sneaking to you?"

"You didn't exactly twist my arm to stay."

"I would have died first. Any man who sneaks out—"

"I didn't sneak!" he repeated, shouting. "I was only being considerate."

"Or cowardly."

"I didn't want to wake you up early on a holiday, when you could sleep in."

"As though I could sleep late after being cramped up on that couch with you all night. Every muscle in my body was sore."

"That wasn't from sleeping," he said, sneering. "That was from the vigorous way you made love."

Her eyes narrowed dangerously. "You didn't seem to mind the way I made love then."

"I didn't. But at least I've got enough guts to admit it."

"I've never denied enjoying Christmas Eve."

He pointed a finger at her. "Just a second ago you denied that you enjoyed sleeping together like a couple of wolf cubs under that fur coat. At the very least you gave a damn good impression of enjoying it. Every time I tried to move away, you whimpered."

"Whimpered? I've never whimpered in my life."

"Oh, no? I'll record us making love one night and play it back to you."

"We won't be making love anymore," she announced dogmatically. "I know I agreed to sleep with you as long as the marriage lasts, but I don't think it's a good idea. And since we don't seem to be able to live together without sleeping together, I think I should move back home."

He threw up his hands. They landed against his thighs with a loud slap. "Oh, great. That's just great. Terrific. As usual, your timing is perfect," he said sarcastically. "No sooner does the article about our marital bliss get published, than the bride skedaddles."

"Bad publicity?"

"You got it."

"That's what has worried you from the very beginning, isn't it? That's why you married me. So your precious mayoral seat wouldn't be jeopardized." She shot him a poisonous look and stalked toward the car.

They sped home in hostile silence. When they arrived, Ria slammed her way through the house. But before she made it to the bedroom door, he caught her shirttail and pulled her up short.

"Let me go, Taylor."

"Uh-uh. Not until we've had this out."

"We've had it out."

"You're reneging on our deal. We agreed to live together as husband and wife . . . in every respect."

"Okay, so I'm not holding up my end of the bargain. No one will know."

"I sure as hell will!"

"You wouldn't if you didn't go around in a perpetual state of arousal."

He backed her into the wall and held her there with his body. His mouth ground a hard, passionate kiss onto hers. When he raised his head he rasped out, "I'm not always horny. Only when I look at you."

She whimpered.

"What do you do to me? Cast a spell?" Ria, sprawled across him, was indolently combing her fingers through his chest hair.

"Whatever it is, we do it to each other."

"You make me lose control."

"It's a damned good thing. I couldn't have held out much longer. I was ready to explode."

Bashfully she rolled her face inward, burying it in the hollow in his rib cage. "You know what I meant."

"Yes, I know." He sighed softly, strumming her spine with his fingertips. "Ria, why did you resign your position at Bishop and Harvey? Did they ask you to?"

"No."

"Urge you to?"

She told him about the problem that the Community Arts Center had raised. "I didn't want to cost the company the contract. And I certainly couldn't let you be accused of conflict of interest. That would be an albatross around your neck for the length of your term as mayor."

Get one full-length Loveswept FREE every month!
Now you can be sure you'll never, ever miss a single
Loveswept title by enrolling in our special reader's home
delivery service. A service that will bring you all six new
Loveswept romances each month for the price of five—and
deliver them to you before they appear in the bookstores!

Examine 6 Loveswept Novels for
15 days FREE!
(SEE OTHER SIDE FOR DETAILS)

"But what about your career? You've worked so hard to get where you are."

She propped her chin on his sternum. "I wasn't lying when I told Delia Starr that I had thought about setting up my own firm for some time."

"You're not just saying that to make me feel better?"

"No. I like my job, but was tired of the intraoffice jealousy, the politics, the infernal grapevine."

"Which we can blame for revealing our secret about the baby. Not that it matters. It would have come out sooner or later."

"Yes, but I thought it would be later. Ideally, after you're sworn in. Delia must have interviewed Guy. I'm sure he told her I was pregnant, to embarrass us."

"Out of spite?"

"Probably. He isn't a very good loser."

"I can't feel sorry for him," Taylor said. "If he'd been all that hot, you wouldn't have gone to bed with me."

"I could say the same for Lisa."

"Before we get into another argument—and frankly, an argument with you plumb wears me out, because it's usually resolved in bed—let's go back to the original subject. Where do you intend to work?"

"At my house. While it's just sitting there unused, I can set myself up in the living room until I find an office for lease. It might be difficult in the beginning, but I believe in myself and my talent. I also believe in Mrs. Graham's word-of-mouth advertising. She's got a lot of friends who are jealous of her new house."

"Starting a new business the same year you're having a baby. Whew! You're a glutton for punishment." He kissed her forehead. "But I believe in you, too, and I'll be willing to help any way I can."

"Thank you, Taylor. I knew you'd be supportive."

"It looks like you've got your career plans all sorted out." He smoothed his hands over her derriere. "What about the other?"

"What other?"

His fingers slipped between her thighs. "About moving out."

"Oh, that." She gazed up at him dreamily. "I'm here, aren't I?"

For Ria, the lovemaking that followed was bittersweet. In the strictest sense of the word, she made love to him. But she knew that it was one-sided. The child she carried was the only thing that truly bound her to him.

Six

Ria let the telephone ring ten times before she finally reached across the bed and answered it.

"Ria, glad I caught you. I was worried."

"Hello, Taylor."

"What's going on?"

"Nothing."

"You went home from work in the middle of the day."

"How did you know I was here?"

"I called your office and they said you'd left for the day. What's up?"

"I just didn't feel like working."

"Why? Ria? Answer me. Is something wrong?"

"No, nothing." She replaced the telephone receiver.

Ten minutes later she heard his car pulling into the driveway. He came barging through the bedroom door, calling her name. For a few seconds he braced himself in the opening, a hand on either side of the jamb. His hair had either been windblown or finger-plowed. He had taken off his suit jacket on the way home or left it behind at his office. Ria hadn't seen him so disheveled since the night she had told him he must marry her.

"What's the matter?" He rushed toward the bed and sat down on the edge of the mattress. His eyes anxiously ranged over her.

"Probably nothing." She tried to smile, but the valiant attempt failed.

"Just a few minutes ago it was 'nothing.' Now it's 'probably nothing.' Which is it? Did you get sick at work?"

Hot, salty tears stung her eyes. She couldn't deal with her own misery and his at the same time, so she turned her face into the pillow. "I started spotting."

Taylor became as still as a buck who scents hunters. Ria couldn't even hear him breathing. Finally he asked hoarsely, "Did you call the doctor?"

"Immediately. He told me to go home to bed. That's what I did."

"That's it? That's all he said? What about medicine?"

"Taylor, there is no medicine for this. No medicine that's been proven to work."

"Dammit, there's gotta be something the doctor can do."

"There is. He's waiting it out, just like I am."

Taylor stood up. Ria remained lying on her side and kept her eyes closed, irrationally afraid that the slightest movement would upset some precarious cosmic balance and she would lose her baby. Taylor paced back and forth at the foot of the bed, casting worried glances down at her.

"I don't know much about this," he said awkwardly. "Exactly what does it mean?"

"It can mean nothing, such as a blood vessel bursting because of increased pressure." She drew a deep breath. "Or it can indicate bleeding from the uterus." If she had seen how drastically Taylor's face paled, she might have stopped there. "Or the placenta might be trying to detach itself."

He swallowed hard. "For the time being the only precaution you can take is to stay in bed?"

"Yes, until the bleeding stops."

"Bleeding? I thought you said spotting."

She rolled over and looked up at him querulously. "What's the difference?"

He sat down beside her again and touched her cheek conciliatorily. "Nothing, I guess. It's just that spotting doesn't sound as bad."

Her lower lip began to tremble, and the tears spilled over her eyelids. "Taylor, I'm scared."

"God, me too. Me too." He clasped her in a bear hug and held on dearly, pressing her face into the notch of his shoulder. "But I'm sure everything will be all right. How often does this happen? All the time, right? Isn't this a fairly common thing? Now that I think about it, it seems to me my stepmother had some difficulty like this with her firstborn, and he's a robust little boy. He runs them ragged now," he said with a forced chuckle.

"The doctor assured me that it's common," Ria said faintly. "There's no reason for alarm unless it gets worse."

"See?" Taylor gently wiped the tears off her cheeks. "Baby just wants that quack to earn the premium fee he's charging to get him here."

She laughed, knowing that he was joking to make her feel better, and hoping that her obligatory laughter would make him feel better. Neither of them was going to feel better until she and the child she carried were completely out of danger.

"Can I get you something? Did you eat lunch?"

She shook her head. "I didn't, but I don't want anything."

"Let me help you out of your clothes."

Her suit was helplessly wrinkled, but she had

just now noticed it. "I didn't even take the time to change. The doctor said to get into bed, and I got."

Taylor helped her undress. When she was down to her underwear, she excused herself and went into the bathroom. While she was behind that closed door, Taylor paced the nap of the carpet down another fraction of an inch. When Ria emerged wrapped in a light cotton robe, she was pale and trembling. Her eyes had lost their green fire and looked as bleak as cold ashes. Her mouth was bruised, as though she'd been biting her lower lip.

"Still?" he asked roughly. She nodded. "No better?"

"No worse."

"Lie back down." He assisted her onto the bed. Her black hair fanned out beneath her head like an inkblot against the white pillowcase. She closed her eyes. Her mascara was smudged. Her lips looked blotched and swollen. There was no bloom in her cheeks. But to Taylor she'd never been more beautiful.

"Does it hurt?"

Her eyes came open slowly. "Not really. It's like having cramps." He nodded solemnly. She smiled and punched him in the arm. "What are you agreeing with, you jerk? You've never had cramps."

He grinned lopsidedly. "I'm damn glad, too. Would an aspirin help?"

"I'd better not take anything without consulting the doctor."

"Are you comfortable? Besides having the, uh, cramps."

"I'm fine. You can go back to your office now. I'll call if I need you."

His brows drew together ominously. "Don't make me mad."

"But Taylor, there's nothing—"

"I'm staying."

Ria fell silent, secretly pleased that he planned to stay with her. She didn't want to face this ordeal alone, no matter what the outcome. If he let go of her hand, she thought she'd fly apart.

"I wish you'd eat something," he said after a moment. "You look all shriveled up."

Ria knew he needed to feel useful, so she sent him after cheese and crackers and fruit juice.

"Taylor?"

"Hm?"

He was sitting on the edge of the bed, staring out the window. Shadows outside were growing longer. The sun was sinking below the horizon.

"What are you thinking?"

"That this is the longest afternoon I've ever lived through." He stroked her cheek. "I know it's been even longer for you."

Ria had sent him on a dozen errands throughout the house. At some point he had realized that these needless errands were a device to keep them both distracted and occupied.

Finally, tacitly, they had agreed to cut out that nonsense. Neither Ria's fickle demands nor Taylor's dogged fetching and carrying was going to take their minds off their child's life, which hung in the balance. There had been long stretches of silence between them, but they were companionable silences. They had communicated their anxiety on a higher plane than conversation would have allowed.

"Whenever we've talked about the baby," Ria began slowly, "it's always been about a healthy baby."

"What are you trying to say?"

"How would you feel about the child if he weren't so healthy? If . . . if he weren't born perfect, how would you feel about him?"

Taylor didn't answer, only looked at her with hard, implacable eyes.

Nervously she went on. "It's the body's natural instinct to try and discard something that isn't perfect. Sometimes a miscarriage should be considered a blessing."

He waited a long time to respond. When he did, it was obvious he was angry. "How could you ask me a question like that? Do you really think I'm that shallow? We didn't know each other very well when we got married, but I thought you knew me better than that now."

Remorseful tears filled her eyes. "I'm sorry, Taylor. You're right. I do know you better than to ask that."

Her tears dissolved his anger. Gently he laid his hands on her stomach, protectively covering her entire lower abdomen with his wide palms and strong fingers. "I love the baby. I want it. No matter what."

She turned her head away, not because she didn't want him to see her tears, but because she couldn't bear to see his.

"I think you'd better take me to the hospital." Standing silhouetted in the open bathroom door, Ria looked on the verge of collapse. She was trembling violently.

Taylor didn't waste time asking unnecessary questions. He'd emptied the bathroom wastepaper basket twice. They no longer had any secrets from each other. He called the doctor and told him they were on their way, then saw to Ria.

He scooped her into his arms and carried her through the house. "Are you in pain?"

"It's not too bad."

It was bad. Her lips were white. He secured her into the front seat of his car, then broke every speed limit and every state and city driving ordinance to reach the hospital. Her OB had arranged for a wheelchair to be waiting outside. As Taylor lowered her into it, she grabbed his hand and pressed it against her tear-damp cheek.

"I'm sorry. I'm so sorry."

The attending orderly didn't give Taylor time to respond before spinning the wheelchair around and pushing it toward the automatic glass doors. Outside the examination room, Taylor fidgeted on the uncomfortable plastic chairs. He sipped rank, vending-machine coffee. He paced. He cursed. He prayed. After what seemed like an eternity, the doctor came out and grimly shook hands with him.

"Hello, Mr. MacKensie. I recognize you from your newspaper pictures."

"How's Ria?"

"I'm afraid she lost the baby."

Taylor sagged against the wall. He had thought he was prepared to hear that, but discovered that he wasn't. The sense of loss was incredible. He felt as though he'd been socked in the gut by a giant fist, and that when it was withdrawn, the hole didn't fill back up, but remained, gaping and empty.

He tilted his head back until it came into contact with the cool tile wall. Eyes closed and teeth bared, he squeezed his hands into fists. "Why?" He asked the question of the Almighty, but it was the doctor who answered him.

"It was certainly nothing that Mrs. MacKensie did or didn't do. Just one of those accidents of nature."

"A blessing," Taylor said bitterly.

"I know it's hard to look at it that way."

"You're right, Doctor. Damned hard." Taylor blew out a long breath. "How is Ria?"

The doctor shook his head pessimistically. "She's extremely upset, naturally. I'm taking her upstairs."

"Upstairs?" The first thing that popped into Taylor's mind was the psychiatric ward. Had Ria gone completely over the edge?

"Yes. Usually the woman's system takes care of discarding the debris on its own, but in this case it didn't and I'm going to do a D and C." He explained the procedure to Taylor.

"She can go home in the morning, but she'll be mildly uncomfortable for a day or two. She should take it easy, do nothing strenuous. Of course our primary concern is for her emotional stability. The emotional wound takes longer to heal than the body, and a lot of the responsibility for that falls to you, Mr. MacKensie."

It was several hours before Ria was moved to a private room and Taylor was allowed to see her. In the interim he called his secretary at home and told her to cancel his appointments for the following day, Friday. He wouldn't be back in his office until after the weekend. He then placed a call to Delia Starr.

"Ria had a miscarriage tonight," he told her as soon as she had answered and he had identified himself.

After a stunned silence the reporter said, "I'm awfully sorry."

"Keep any reference to the baby out of that damned feature story Sunday."

"It's too late for that, Taylor."

"The hell it is."

"I've already turned the piece over to the copy editors. It's out of my hands."

"Then get it back. I won't let Ria open up the paper and read about the baby she's not going to have. I don't care what you need to do, just do it."

"I'll do what I can." Knowing the power that Ms. Starr wielded in the city room, that was as good as a promise that any and all references to the child would be edited out before press time.

Taylor also got the word of the hospital's chief of staff that nothing about Ria should be leaked to the media. Mayor-elect MacKensie was news. This was one time Taylor didn't want to read any mention of himself on the front page of the newspaper.

Ria's hospital room was dark and shadowy. Only one small night light was burning. Taylor thought she was sleeping, but as he crept nearer the bed, he saw that her eyes were open. Unmoving, she was staring at the ceiling. Her right hand looked frail and bloodless where it lay on her stomach, which looked obscenely concave.

She turned her head, but said nothing. Taylor could think of nothing to say that didn't sound banal. Did tragedy automatically reduce normally articulate people to robots who were programmed to say only the expected things? He finally settled for, "How do you feel?"

"Empty."

The tonelessness of her voice alarmed him. It had died, just as her smile and animation had. He lifted her hand off her stomach and closed his fingers around it tightly, but she seemed not to notice. She didn't return his squeeze.

"I exercise in a health club for hours each week just to keep my tummy flat." She laughed mirthlessly. "Mom always said, 'Be careful what you wish for.'" Taylor saw tears leave the outer corners of her eyes and roll toward the pillow. Her dark hair absorbed them.

"Are you in pain?"

'No. The doctor ordered a shot to help me sleep. That's why I'm so woozy."

"Be woozy. The doctor said you'd need plenty of rest."

"He also said that there was no reason why I couldn't have other . . . other . . ." She became so choked up, she couldn't speak.

Taylor bent over her, propping his arm on the headboard and tightly squeezing the hand he held. "Don't, Ria. Don't cry anymore. Go to sleep."

"I can't stop thinking about the baby." Her voice was gritty with emotion. "It isn't there anymore. It doesn't exist."

"Shh." Taylor kissed her eyelids closed, though tears continued to roll down her temples. He pulled a chair up to the bed, sat down, and didn't move from her side until the sedative had taken effect and she fell asleep.

In fact the sun was coming up before he left her. He stopped by the nurses' station and issued strict instructions that Ria be given anything she needed. Then he went home, showered, shaved, and quickly ate a scrambled egg. He scarfed it down ravenously, since he hadn't eaten anything since lunch the day before. He fortified himself with several cups of scalding black coffee before returning to the hospital, taking a change of clothes for Ria with him.

He stopped in the lobby gift shop to buy her some flowers. He had wanted roses, but they only had red ones, and they reminded him unpleasantly of blood. He rejected pink carnations because they symbolized baby girls. He left with a bouquet of yellow daisy mums, which he decided looked cheerful, at least. As soon as he stepped off the elevator, he saw Ria's doctor in the corridor outside her room.

"I've just examined her," he told Taylor. "Physically she's doing fine, but she's very depressed. The sooner she can resume her normal routine, the better. I told her to come see me in six weeks."

He was off. Taylor wanted to grab him by the flapping tails of his white lab coat and ask a thousand questions, but he wanted to see Ria more.

With her suitcase in one hand, flowers in the other, he entered her room. She was dabbling a spoon into a bowl of lumpy gray oatmeal that a starving man *might* have been talked into eating.

"I can do better than that," he said, nodding down toward her breakfast tray. He laid the bouquet beside it and set the suitcase on the floor. "You've never had my superduper Belgian waffles, have you?"

She smiled wanly. "Thank you for the flowers. And for bringing my clothes."

"I hope I brought everything you need."

Pushing the unwanted tray away, she swung her legs over the side of the bed. Taylor stifled an impulse to spring to her assistance as she stood up. "I've already showered, so I won't be a minute." He got the message. He wasn't invited to stay and help her dress.

"I'll take care of all the release forms," he said, backing toward the door.

"I've already signed them."

"I want to settle the account."

"It's paid. I took care of that too."

Taylor's mouth thinned with irritation. "You've been a busy lady this morning."

"Excuse me, please," she said coldly. "I want to dress and get out of here."

When she came out of the room a few minutes later, her lipstick looked exceptionally bright and garish in contrast to her pallor. The wheelchair should have melted beneath the baleful look she gave it.

"I can leave under my own steam."

"Their rules, not mine." Taylor, not the nurse, had his hands on the back of the chair. And he, not the nurse, indicated with a brusque nod of his head for Ria to sit down in it. He'd just about reached the end of his patience.

Once they were in the car Ria said, "You can drop me at my house. I'll come over later to pack my things." Taylor deliberately drove past the turn. "Did you hear what I said?"

"I heard, but I didn't listen."

Ria jerked her head forward. "Suit yourself. This will work out better anyway, because I need to get my car. I can do it all in one fell swoop."

He turned up the volume on the radio and tonelessly sang along.

When he stopped the car, he tried to rush ahead of Ria, helping her out of the car, opening doors, but she seemed determined to do things by herself, and spurned his efforts to help her. Once inside the house, she went directly to the bedroom closet. Lifting several hangers off the bar, she carried them to the bed. Just when she was about to drop the first folded dress into the opened suitcase, Taylor stepped forward and yanked the garment out of her hand.

"Just what the hell is going on with you? What do you think you're doing?"

"Give me back my dress. I'm packing."

"Why?"

"I'm moving back home."

"For the last few weeks this has been your home."

"It had reason to be. That reason is now wrapped in a plastic bag and lying in a trash dumpster behind the hospital."

The moment the angrily shouted words left her mouth, she clapped her hands across it and slumped down onto the edge of the bed. "Oh,

God." Groaning, she covered her face with her hands.

For several minutes she rocked back and forth, silently mourning. Then she lowered her hands and looked up at Taylor. "I'm sorry. That was a ghastly thing to say." She drew in several deep breaths and nervously wiped her hands on her skirt. "Taylor, you've been wonderful about everything. Yesterday. Last night. This morning. It was sweet of you to bring me flowers." She glanced at the partially wilted mums now lying on the bed, where she had negligently tossed them when she came in.

"I want to thank you for showing so much consideration and patience, Taylor. But . . . but the reason we got married in the first place no longer exists." She blinked away the flow of tears. "The doctor told me that I should resume my normal routine as soon as possible. Under the circumstances that means— "

She glanced up and was shocked to discover that she was talking to an empty room.

Taylor sometimes had a social drink at lunch, if he was entertaining a client and the client wanted one. But he never drank before ten o'clock in the morning. So when that first fiery belt of Scotch landed in his stomach, he sucked in a sharp breath and blinked tears out of his eyes. Just to prove that he could, he drained the glass of Scotch before stepping out onto the patio.

It, like everything else around the place, had undergone a facelift, otherwise known as Ria's touch. There were well-tended hanging baskets and clay pots of blooming flowers everywhere. He'd had blooming flowers on his patio before, but by the middle of the summer they were either brown from not getting enough water or yellow from getting too much or straggling because he'd forgotten to pinch them back.

This year his flowers were hothouse-pretty and flourishing. They typified the improvements Ria had made since she'd moved in. Not that she'd started changing things helter-skelter, like the dingbat mistress in a Neil Simon comedy. She always asked his permission before moving a chair a few inches one way or the other.

The alterations she'd made ranged from dramatic, such as hanging her cherished Erte lithograph over the fireplace in the bedroom, to subtle, such as keeping fresh flowers on the dining table. All her changes were improvements, not impositions. He couldn't walk through his house, which had been a showplace before, without seeing traces of Ria on everything. Her stamp was as indelible as the red letters on first-class postage.

Hell, it was a cliché, but she'd made his house a home and given it a woman's touch. It had been spectacular when the expensive decorator got through with it. Now it was spectacular and homey. Ria had added what no decorator could—warmth. She'd breathed personality into the beautiful rooms. She was its heart.

He'd gotten accustomed to seeing her nightgown hanging on the hook inside the bathroom door. He'd even been guilty of fondling it every time he went in or out, of holding it against his nose and breathing in her scent, like a druggie getting secret fixes throughout the day.

He hadn't minded seeing her razor resting next to his. In fact, he'd thought it was kinda cute. Pink. With impressions of daisies on it.

"Hell." He spat out the terse expletive and crammed his fists into his pockets. Out of pure meanness, he kicked a crimson geranium. What the hell was he doing, thinking about razors with daisies on them? He'd gone daffy.

Still, he couldn't help but think of her dressing table. It was lined with perfume atomizers that made air freshener unnecessary. The scores of little glass jars intrigued him. Silver-capped rouge pots held everything imaginable except rouge. He'd spent one entire, entertaining evening investigating them, asking her what this or that was for, sniffing it, rubbing the creamy contents between his fingers, and remembering times when he'd smelled or felt or tasted that particular emulsion somewhere on Ria's body. She was so deliciously feminine. He was going to miss having that feminine element in the house.

"Face it," he said with a growl to the wounded geranium, "I'm going to miss *her*."

He'd never lacked for female companionship, but there was something to be said for coming home to the same woman every night. It was much more relaxed than dating. Conversation came naturally; it wasn't a skill that constantly had to be practiced.

When they went out in public he never had to wonder if his "date" was going to be dressed to suit the occasion, because Ria always was. She never committed a faux pas. She always knew the right thing to say in any social situation.

Dropping down onto a chaise, Taylor contemplated the horizon through the tent he made of his fingers. How could he convince her to stay?

He wasn't just considering himself, either, he thought righteously. He was being considerate of her. Damn, she'd looked pale and hollow when they left the hospital. And more than just physically wasted. She'd been emptied out spiritually, too.

Yes, she needed to get back into her routine. But if he knew her, and he felt as though he were coming to know her fairly well, she'd drive herself until she collapsed from exhaustion. Deep down she was probably blaming herself for the miscarriage. By now she'd probably remembered some childhood transgression that had finally caught up with her. She would convince herself that the miscarriage had been her penance.

"I'll be damned before I let that happen."

Taylor left the patio and went storming through the house. Halfway to the bedroom, he brought himself up short. This was the wrong approach. A smart man didn't issue ultimatums to Ria Lavender. If he went in there barking orders, that was the last he'd see of her. On the other hand, if he told her that he wanted to take care of her until she was completely recovered, she'd resent his pity. So what was it to be?

Firm but sympathetic. Yeah, that should do it.

He paused on the threshold of the bedroom. She had filled one suitcase and was folding clothing into another one. He felt the whiskey in his stomach heave and swell like the north Atlantic.

He didn't want to use his ace in the hole to get her to stay, but he would if nothing else worked.

Ria turned at the sound of his approach. She mistook the glitter in his eyes for anger. She couldn't really blame him, not after the dreadful thing she'd said. He would welcome her leaving as soon as possible. "Give me another minute or two. I only need to pack my cosmetics in the bathroom, then I'll be ready."

"I don't think you should leave."

Dropping a lacy teddy into the suitcase, she spun around. "What?"

"You heard me."

"But why?"

"The doctor said you needed bed rest, at least through the weekend."

"I've got a bed at home."

"But will you stay in it?"

"Yes."

"Uh-huh."

"I will!"

"Ria, I've lived with you for several weeks. As long as there's an unwashed glass in the kitchen sink, you won't sit down to watch a television program."

She avoided looking at him, partially because she was guilty as charged and partially because he was so devastatingly good to look at. His lack of sleep the night before had only emphasized the bone structure of his face. Fatigue flattered him. The shadows around his eyes made them appear a deeper blue.

He was dressed in a trim-fitting sport shirt that showed off the triangular shape of his torso. The faded, tight jeans looked as though they had been melted down and poured over him. It seemed impossible that that fit could have been achieved by any other method.

The hurting emptiness inside her yawned wider when she thought of not having him in her life. She was going to miss his humor. And his passion.

"I promise I'll rest," she said lamely.

"You need to eat properly. You won't if I'm not around to force-feed you."

"How do you know?"

"I saw your oatmeal bowl this morning."

"It was horrible. You wouldn't have eaten it either."

"I didn't have to."

"I can cook well-balanced meals for myself."

"Precisely. You shouldn't be standing up cooking, much less going to the market."

"I won't starve, Taylor. You make me sound like an invalid. I got along very well for almost thirty years without you." He wouldn't have a comeback for that, and she knew it.

He took another tack. "What are you going to tell your parents?"

"Oh." Her triumphant smile collapsed. "I had forgotten that."

"Good thing I reminded you, then. They're driving down on Sunday to meet me, aren't they?"

"I'll call and tell them something came up."

"It would be out of character for you to break an important date like that. They'd figure out that something was wrong, probably drive down anyway to find out what it was, and then, when they got here and discovered—"

"All right!" She sank down onto the bed. Her shoulders slumped dejectedly. Packing had exhausted her. The doctor was right. She couldn't just pick up where she had left off. It would take time to build her strength back up, especially when her spirits were so low. "I suppose I could stay here until Sunday night, after Mom and Dad leave. I'll think up something to tell them about us later."

"Actually," Taylor said, sitting down beside her, "I think you should stay for a . . . a while."

"Indefinitely?"

"Yeah."

"Why?"

He shrugged. "Lots of reasons."

"Name one."

"You just got here," he said shortly.

"And what will people say if I move out right now? Isn't that what you're getting at?"

"No, Ria."

"Isn't it?" She sprang to her feet. "I get it now. All this talk about resting, eating properly, sparing my folks, is just so much bunk. You don't want your voting public to know that your new wife walked out on you."

"You know that's not why I want you to stay."

"And if they found out that I'd lost a baby, that would really make you look bad, wouldn't it? They might not be too excited about swearing you in as mayor."

"My being mayor has nothing to do with why I want you to stay."

"Then it must be the free sex."

"What?" he roared. The tethers he'd kept on his temper snapped.

"Sure, why should you spend money taking out Lisa and her ilk, when you can have a bedmate at home every night for free?"

"I've never known you to have a convenient headache," he said.

"Not until now," she ground out. "But for your information, I'm off limits for six weeks."

His curses were so vivid, so vile, they made Ria shudder. "What do you think I am, a caveman? Is that what you think this is about? Sex? Ha! Don't flatter yourself. I had plenty of it, for *free*, before Christmas Eve. That wasn't the first one-night stand I'd ever had, you know." He jerked his chin up arrogantly. "Or even the best one."

That smarted, as though he'd slapped her. But rather than let him know he'd hurt her, she asked, "Then why do you want to stay married to me?"

"To save face," he said bluntly. "Stay with me until I'm officially sworn in as mayor. Then if you want to leave, I won't try to stop you. I think you owe me that much."

Ria's strength and defiance deserted her in the same instant. She sat down on the bed again. Idly she picked through the suitcase of frilly underwear, remembering one of Taylor's bawdy comments for nearly every garment.

More than any pain she'd endured, this hurt. Their marriage had been a sham. These past weeks he hadn't been falling in love with her, as she had been with him. He'd been kind, funny, and considerate only for the baby's sake. He had been affectionate only because she was the mother of his child. His possessive attitude had nothing to do with her personally.

And they'd always been very good for each other in bed.

He'd acknowledged and legitimized her baby by marrying her, just as she'd asked him to. He hadn't only been a good sport about it; he'd gone out of his way to make her feel like a well-loved bride.

It would be unsportsmanlike of her to leave him in the lurch now. His career depended on his public image. She'd got him into this marriage, making as little fuss as possible. It was up to her to get him out of it the same way.

But could she bear pretending to be his loving wife? When would he realize that she wasn't pretending? How much longer was it until the swearing-in ceremony? Several weeks? A month?

She supposed she could endure living with him for that long.

The deciding factor, however, was that the thought of leaving him was so dismal, she really couldn't bring herself to do it.

"All right, Taylor. I'll stay."

Seven

"More coffee, Frida?" Taylor leaned down to pour his mother-in-law another cup. They were enjoying their after-dinner coffee on the patio.

Mrs. Lavender smiled up at him. "Are you trying to butter me up?"

"Naturally," he confessed with a wide grin. "I want to make a good first impression."

His parents-in-law laughed at his disarming honesty. At Robert Lavender's urging, Taylor began outlining some of the city-improvement programs he wanted to initiate once he was sworn into office.

Ria, feet drawn up onto the chaise, watched the three of them. The day had gone well, far better than Ria had had any right to expect. She had dreaded it, dreaded having to deceptively play the role of a happy newlywed for the two people she loved and respected most.

The moment she had answered the front door to her parents that morning, tears had threatened. She'd been tempted to throw herself into their arms and have a good cry, pouring out the whole sordid story. At least she hadn't had to talk about the miscarriage. One of the wisest decisions she'd ever made had been not to tell them about her pregnancy. They would be upset when her short-lived marriage ended in annulment. Why distress them further by telling them about the grandchild they had lost?

Credit for the day's going so smoothly went to Taylor. It was no mystery to Ria why he had been elected mayor. He was a born politician. He was charming and gracious, a wonderful conversationalist, and an even better listener. If he was faking his sincerity, then he was a superb actor. There were times when even she was convinced that he liked her parents and wanted them to like him. He could have won a Son-in-law of the Year contest hands down.

He was also a model husband. She couldn't fault his performance in that role. What depressed her was that it was just that, a role.

Their argument Friday afternoon over whether she would stay or go taxed her already depleted strength. Once they had replaced all her clothing in the closet, Taylor had ordered her to bed, and she had obeyed without argument. She'd slept most of that day away. He had brought her a supper tray to the bedroom. As soon as she'd eaten, she fell asleep again.

Waking up Saturday morning, she'd noticed that his side of the bed hadn't been slept in. Tiptoeing through the house, she'd found him sprawled half on, half off the living-room sofa. It had pricked her conscience to think that she had forced him out of his own bed. She'd decided to make amends by cooking breakfast.

A few minutes later he had stumbled into the kitchen, where she already had the coffee maker going. "What are you doing up?" He had haphazardly wrapped a sheet around his middle and was clutching it with one hand while scratching his tousled head with the other. He yawned broadly.

"Making coffee. You look like you need some."

"Go back to bed. I'll bring you yours."

"I feel fine."

"Go back to bed or—"

"I'm—"

"—I'll drop this sheet and expose myself to you. And you know what happens to me first thing every morning whether I want it or not," he warned softly.

She scuttled back to bed. The coffee he brought her was accompanied by three strips of crisp bacon and the largest waffle she'd ever seen. Its corners overlapped the plate.

"Why don't we stuff this and use it for a throw pillow?"

Her joke didn't amuse him. He picked up a fork and folded her fingers around it. "Eat it. Every bite." She could manage only half the waffle before surrendering with pleas of mercy.

So it went all day. He wouldn't let her do anything for herself. When she complained about going stir-crazy in the bedroom, he let her lie on a chaise in the sun on the patio.

From there she got to watch him wash and wax both cars. Wearing only denim cut-offs and splattered car-wash suds, he kept her from getting much rest. Her eyes kept straying from her magazine to those clumps of soapy white foam that clung to his chest hair and sensuously slid down his bare thighs and calves. She'd never seen anybody make an art form out of dripping water, the way Taylor did.

"I'm going to the grocery store. What should we serve our guests for lunch tomorrow?" Note pad in hand, he plopped down on the foot of her chaise, straddling it and facing her.

Ria was glad he had exchanged the damp cut-offs for slacks. The sight was disquieting enough as it was. She hoped he couldn't see the direction of her gaze behind her sunglasses.

"I hadn't thought about it," she said, doing so now. "How about chicken crepes, a huge green salad, parsley carrots, and strawberry tarts?"

"Let's see," he said, writing on the pad, "that's cold sliced ham and potato salad from the deli, fresh fruit and Brie, French bread and butter. Good idea, Ria. And I think the sherbet sounds delicious for dessert. Which should it be, orange or lime?"

"Taylor!"

"I'll grill steaks out here on the patio for dinner. Baking potatoes is no hassle." He laid a finger against her protesting lips. "But if you're a very good girl and stay off your feet for the rest of today, I'll let you make that 'huge green salad' tomorrow."

The spontaneous kiss he dropped on her mouth surprised them both. For a moment they stared at each other. Then he said a gruff good-bye and left quickly.

The next morning, before the Lavenders arrived, they read Delia Starr's feature article on them. "There's nothing in here about the baby," Ria remarked, faintly surprised by the omission.

"I made certain there wouldn't be."

Ria laid the paper in her lap. "When?"

"I called her from the hospital. I knew you wouldn't want to make public or private explanations."

"Thank you, Taylor." She reached out and touched his shoulder. He covered her hand with his.

And now, all day, they'd played house for her parents' benefit. It was beginning to grate on Ria's nerves. Because at times, she forgot it was play-acting. Taylor was attentive, leaping to her side every time she lifted anything heavier than a feather. Once, when she bent down to pick up a fallen napkin from the floor, he nearly knocked her over trying to get to it first.

"Will you relax?" she said in a strident whisper, having called him into the kitchen on some pretext.

"Will you stop doing things you shouldn't?"

"They don't know about the . . . the baby." She still couldn't bring herself to say the word *miscarriage.* "They'll get suspicious if you don't stop behaving like a fool."

"They think I'm a fool in love, waiting on his bride hand and foot."

"Well your enthusiasm is driving me crazy. Stop it."

But he didn't. He was constantly near her, touching her cheek, massaging her neck, rubbing the small of her back, placing a solicitous arm around her. Once, for no apparent reason, he bent down and kissed her lips softly. She felt a flurry in her tummy before remembering that his demonstrations of affection were calculated and a part of the show.

"Ria? Did you hear what I said?"

She pulled herself out of her musings to find that all of them were staring at her curiously. "I'm sorry. What did you say?"

Taylor instantly moved to her side. "Are you all right?" His blue eyes seemed to spear straight through hers.

"I'm fine. I just lost track of the conversation. Repeat what you said, Dad."

"I said that I'm glad you didn't marry that stuffed shirt Guy Whatshisname."

"You and me both, Robert," Taylor said, curling his hand around the back of Ria's neck.

Frida Lavender said, "I guess it's safe to tell you now, Ria, that your father and I never liked Guy much. Taylor is much more suited to your personality." She gazed at them affectionately. "I think it's so romantic that you met on Christmas Eve."

"Yes, it was," Ria said uneasily.

"I guess it was fated that we took that trip to London when we did," Mr. Lavender said.

Taylor covered his heart with his hand. "Then I shall be eternally grateful to fate."

They laughed, but Frida's pretty mouth puckered into a frown. "We would have liked being at your wedding. It was so sudden. It hardly seems official without the church and organ and flowers. All the trimmings."

"Mom, I—"

"My fault entirely," Taylor said, interrupting Ria. "Ria and I had talked marriage from the night we met." He smiled down at her and added sexily, "It was that kind of night." He held her gaze for a moment before addressing her parents again. "When I finally convinced her to marry me, I suggested that we do it right away and as quietly as possible. Please forgive us, but I didn't want my rivals to think I was grandstanding for the sake of the election, since my bachelorhood had been such an issue.

"And"—he paused, to stress the importance of his words—"the exchanging of vows meant something so personal and special to Ria and me, we selfishly didn't want to share them."

Mrs. Lavender blinked, misty-eyed. "Ria's very lucky to have found a man with your sensitivity, Taylor MacKensie."

Robert Lavender reached for his wife's hand. "Time to go. If she starts crying, there'll be no stopping her. Besides, we've got that hundred-mile drive facing us."

Standing together in the doorway, arms around each other's waists, Taylor and Ria made promises she knew they would never keep, about going to visit her parents soon and allowing them to host a dinner party so they could introduce Taylor to all their friends.

By the time the taillights of their car disappeared down the street, her nerves were shot. She closed the door with more emphasis than was necessary. "You didn't have to overdo it, you know," she snapped.

Taylor was taken aback. "I thought I did an admirable job of convincing them that I was a loving, attentive husband."

"Oh, you did. Every word was as syrupy-sweet as that waffle you forced me to eat yesterday."

"So what are you complaining about?"

She placed her hands on her hips. "Shouldn't you have been just a smidgen less charming? Somewhat of a heel? At the very least a little inattentive? They're going to be shocked when the big split comes. They'll ask themselves how I could be stupid enough to let Sir Galahad slip through my fingers. They might be relieved when we break up, if you'd shown one single dastardly flaw today instead of being so damned *perfect*."

"Well, excuse me. Next time I'll try to act more like stuffed-shirt Guy."

"They didn't know him well or they wouldn't have called him that."

"They knew him well enough not to like him. But you damn sure did, didn't you?"

"Yes."

"How long were you with him? And just what has he got that made you so dotty over him, when nobody else even likes him?" His blue eyes glittered. "Or shouldn't I ask?"

She tossed back her hair and airily replied, "You shouldn't ask."

Cursing, Taylor went stamping toward the garage. "I'm going jogging."

As soon as she heard the back door slam behind him, Ria's proud posture collapsed. She was tired. Trying to appear healthy and happy had exhausted her. Trying to hide her feelings for Taylor had strained her nerves to the breaking point.

If she hated him, if he had ever given her reason to hate him, pretending to love him would have been a challenging game. As it was, she continually had to remind herself that none of their affection or intimacy meant anything.

By the time he came in, she was already in bed. She played possum when he went into the bathroom and closed the door. Moments later she heard the shower running.

Oh, Lord, what a mess she'd made of things.

When he left the bathroom, she did her best to silence her sobs, but something tipped him off. He halted on his way through the bedroom door, changed direction, and moved toward the bed. He bridged her head with his arms.

"Ria? Are you crying? Is something wrong?" She shook her head, but he wasn't convinced. "It's not . . . you're not bleeding excessively or anything, are you?" He flung the sheet back and turned her onto her back.

"No, it's nothing like that." She rubbed the tears off her cheeks, but not before the moonlight shone on them.

"You are crying."

"As I've done for three days solid," she said with self-disgust. "I never cry. Recently that's all I do."

"You're entitled. The doctor warned me that you would be pretty upset for a week or so."

He was wearing only a towel around his hips. His hair, still wet, clung to his head adorably. His chest hair was damp and curly. That silky thatch around his navel had drops of water nestling in it. Because he was using his arms to support himself, the muscles and veins in his bicepses bulged.

Ria wanted to kiss his mouth, his neck, his nipples, which the cool room had made erect. She wanted to catch each glistening drop of water on his body with her tongue and swallow his clean taste along with it. Since she couldn't do any of those things, she started to cry again.

"What's the matter?" Baffled, he lowered himself to her side and pulled her into his arms. "Look, I'm sorry I yelled at you. It's been a rough day for me too."

"I shouldn't have put you through it."

"I asked to be put through it, remember? And I didn't mean what I said about Guy. Well, I meant it—I don't like him either—but I'm sorry it hurt your feelings." He was speaking earnestly enough, but saying all the wrong things. He was ineffectually brushing back her hair, but mostly succeeding only in poking his fingers into her eyes.

Suddenly Ria found the situation absurd, and she began to laugh and cry at the same time. "I've made such a mess of things," she said, blubbering.

"Like what?"

"Your life."

"Huh?"

"Taylor, hasn't it occurred to you that if I'd just waited a few more weeks, you wouldn't have been involved at all?" He held the corner of the sheet against her face. Dutifully she wiped away her tears. "I'd have lost the baby and you never would have been the wiser. But no, I had to come bull-dozing my way into your life, demanding that you marry me."

"Come, now, you're much more like a butterfly than a bulldozer."

"Don't patronize me."

Smiling, he pressed her head against his furry, naked chest. "Hasn't it occurred to you how re-sponsible I feel for ruining your life? I got you pregnant."

"We both got me pregnant."

"But I should have been wearing something. Barring that, I should have withdrawn before . . . you know."

They were both still for a very long time. Finally Ria whispered, "I don't think I'd have let you do that."

"Maybe not that first time. It happened so fast."

"We lost our heads. Weren't thinking."

"But the second time. And the third." He sank his fingers into her hair and began massaging her scalp. "We had plenty of time to think respon-sibly, and we didn't."

Yes, both those times had been slow and lan-guid lovemaking. As his body had stroked hers, they'd gazed into each other's eyes, marveling over how wonderful it felt, gliding into a sweet oblivion together.

Ria tactfully changed the subject. "It's too late for recriminations about Christmas Eve."

"But not about our honeymoon."

"Honeymoon?"

"These last three weeks. Ria, was there a night when we didn't make love?"

"No."

"And that's not counting the mornings and the nooners, and—" He broke off and ran a hand down his face. "It's no wonder you lost the baby."

"Oh, Taylor, don't." She raised up and clasped his face between her hands. "The doctor said that nothing could have prevented the miscarriage because nothing in particular caused it."

"Not even a marathon of sex?"

"No. Especially not sex with you. I mean," she added hastily, "you've never been rough."

"I never hurt you?"

"Of course not." She replaced her head on his chest and hugged him tightly.

He sighed with relief. "I didn't think so. I didn't intend to. But when you lost the baby, I was afraid that I'd been hurting you and you just hadn't said anything."

"No, no." She shook her head from side to side, as much to make her point as to feel his chest hair brushing back and forth across her face and lips.

"I've been so worried about that."

"See? That's what I mean," she said. "You shouldn't have had to worry about any of this. I wish I had never involved you. This is such a landmark in your life and career."

"Our marriage hasn't affected my career anything like it's affected yours."

"I told you I wanted to go into business for myself."

"And I told you that our marriage was a plus to my public image."

"But because of me you haven't been able to enjoy your success. I've interfered with every area of your life. If I'd left you alone, your relationship with Lisa wouldn't have suffered this setback."

"What about your relationship with Guy?"

"Frankly?"

"Frankly."

"It wasn't going anywhere anyway."

She wished he'd say the same thing about his

relationship with Lisa, but he didn't. She wished she had the courage to refuse his comfort, but she didn't. Having his arms around her was a luxury she felt she deserved after the past few days. She luxuriated in the closeness and wanted to prolong it for as long as possible.

"Taylor, what did you do with all the books?"

"The baby books?"

"Uh-huh."

"I put them away so you wouldn't see them. I thought they might upset you."

"They would have. Thank you."

Leaning back against the headboard, he stroked her hair, rearranging the dark, heavy strands across his stomach. "Your folks are great."

"You think so?"

"Yes. You take after your mother."

"I'm adopted, remember? If I resemble her, it's a coincidence."

"Not so much physically. I meant mannerisms, patterns of speech. That kind of thing. And I really like your Dad."

"Is he anything like yours?"

"No, not really. About the same age, though."

Ria absently plucked at his chest hair. "Taylor, are you jealous of your stepsister and stepbrother?"

"No. They're just kids. Cute kids. Good kids."

She lifted her head and looked at him. "You have every right to be jealous. You don't have as much of your father as you would if it weren't for them." Absently she raked her thumbnail over his lips.

"I know he loved my mother. I know he loves me. It's just that his new family needs him now more than I do."

"But?"

"But sometimes I'm jealous," he said with a self-deprecating laugh. "Do you think I'm a jerk?"

"Perfectly normal."

When she realized that her thumb was still caressing his lips, she removed it. He looked down at her mouth. Ria felt a familiar and welcomed heat spreading through her. It proved that she had survived and was still functioning. It was the first time she'd felt alive and warm in days. Apparently Taylor wasn't immune to it. He eased her away from him.

"I'd better let you get some sleep." He swung his legs over the side of the bed and stood up. "Good night, Ria."

"Taylor." She reached out and caught his arm. He turned and looked down at her. Self-consciously she snatched her hand back. "I can't sleep, knowing how uncomfortable you are in there on the sofa." She lowered her eyes, not wanting him to see how close she was to begging. "What I mean is, if you want to sleep in here, it's fine with me."

"In here? In the same bed?"

"Yes. Nothing can happen, right?"

"Right. Absolutely."

"So why shouldn't we be comfortable?"

What each was thinking but neither voiced was that sleeping that close together might be more uncomfortable than not. Yet they didn't want to deny themselves the reassuring nearness of the other.

"Well, if you're sure."

"I'm sure."

Ria lay back down and pulled the sheet and blanket over her shoulders. She closed her eyes. Holding her breath, she heard the wet towel land softly on the carpet. Listening to his naked body sliding between the sheets made her heart pound. The thought of all that warm, hair-smattered skin lying sandwiched between the cool, smooth sheets kept her awake and tense. She held her body rigid for fear of accidentally touching him with her foot. When he spoke her name from out of the darkness, she actually jumped.

"What?"

"Ria, I'm very sorry about the baby."

She could feel his hand searching for hers. Instinctively she reached out and latched onto it. He squeezed her hand tightly. "So am I, Taylor. Very sorry."

"Do you still think about him?"

"Yes."

"I do too." After a lengthy pause he said, "You'll probably have another baby someday."

"Yes, maybe. And so will you."

"Yeah, maybe."

Neither sounded too enthusiastic or optimistic. But they silently acknowledged that they stood a better chance of warding off their sadness together rather than individually, so their hands remained clasped under the covers.

"Ria?"

"Hm?"

Sleepily she turned toward her husband, who cuddled her against him. He nuzzled her face, then kissed her lips. Ria loved these first-thing-in-the-morning kisses, when his beard lightly scraped her skin. She draped an arm across his waist. Her lips were pliant beneath his. His tongue slid between them and touched hers. She sighed and kneed him gently in the groin. He was swollen and hot.

Fumbling for her breast, he grumbled, "How come you've got on a nightgown?"

He managed to unfasten the pearl buttons on the chemise-style nightgown. Her full breast fell into his seeking hand. He massaged it, loving the way its round plumpness reshaped itself to fit his palm. He whisked his thumb over the crest. Again. It beaded.

"Taylor . . ."

"Hm?"

"Nothing. I was just sighing your name because that feels so good."

He groaned. "I want you bad, baby."

As they kissed, Ria nudged his middle with hers, then stayed to rub against him in a mating rhythm. Their open mouths melded. He sent his tongue deep, burying it in the hot, sweet cocoon of her mouth.

Rolling on top of her, his lips traveled down her neck to her breasts. He kissed them through the sheer cotton, then rooted against them until his lips touched bare skin. Drowsily his tongue caressed her nipple.

Ecstasy rippled through Ria. When his lips closed around her nipple and he began to suck, she shivered in delight. It seemed that the invisible nerve fiber connecting breast to womb was more finely tuned than usual. Her lower body contracted hungrily with each gentle tug of his mouth.

Her eyes came open slowly. She ran her fingers up through his mussed hair. She parted her thighs. He moved between them.

Suddenly she woke up fully. "Taylor!"

"Now? Oh, yes, sweetheart, yes."

He framed her face between his hands and kissed her passionately. His lower body frantically rocked against hers. Panties were something he'd never had to deal with in their bed, especially first thing in the morning.

"Taylor."

"Hm?" He was kissing her madly. His hips were thrusting wildly.

"We're making love."

"God, yes, I know."

She grasped double handfuls of hair and pulled his head up. He blinked himself awake. When realization dawned, he rolled to his side and stared at her in speechless dismay. With her hair tousled, the flounced hem of her nightgown bunched up around her waist, the gaping bodice exposing more rosy, ripe breast than it was covering, and the debauched fullness to her lips, she looked like the soiled dove in a Victorian novel—as desirable as she was forbidden.

Glancing down at his aroused sex, he muttered a curse. Rolling off the bed, he stumbled into the bathroom.

"Nothing happened, really. You were still asleep. I know you didn't mean to," Ria said shyly as she handed him a cup of coffee half an hour later.

"I don't want to talk about it." He burned his tongue on the coffee, and cursed it viciously.

"I just don't want you to think that I think that you did it intentionally."

"I didn't do it intentionally."

"That's what I just said."

"Then what are you shouting about?"

"I wasn't shouting until you started shouting."

"Look," he said, slicing the air with his free hand, "a guy wakes up in his own bed and there's a naked girl in it—"

"I was not naked."

"Okay, an almost-naked girl."

"And I'm not a *girl*, either. I'm your wife."

"Then you can't blame me for treating you like a wife, can you?"

"I don't."

"There's just no reasoning with you, Ria. I'm going to be late." He yanked his suit coat off the kitchen chair, which went flying backward. Picking up his briefcase, he stormed out. Seconds after the door slammed behind him, he shoved it open and stuck his head inside. "Don't do anything stupid today, like climb a mountain. Take it easy."

The dishes rattled a second time when he shut the door.

His telling her not to do anything turned out to be superfluous. She got the sum total of nothing accomplished. Her mind wouldn't stay on a single project. Ideas weren't creeping into her head, much less springing. She couldn't attribute her lack of productivity to postweekend ennui, or even to the miscarriage. Physically she felt almost normal.

Her mind was preoccupied with her quasi-marriage. If they had many more scenes like the one that morning, she and Taylor would end up murdering each other, or sorely wanting to.

Surely he would agree with her now that it would be better for them both if she moved out and they got a quiet annulment. He was beyond being crippled politically. The newspapers were filled with stories about him and how his energetic leadership would benefit the city. He wouldn't be affected by the break nearly as much as Ria would.

She'd fallen in love with him. Living with him while knowing that their marriage was on death row was more than she could stand. It would be much better for her peace of mind to close this chapter of her life now. Staying would only result in falling more deeply in love with him, or hating him for not loving her back. Both were bleak prospects.

Having discovered that their tempers seemed to be directly linked to their libidos, Ria decided to approach him calmly and coolly. She even had a cold beer waiting for him when he came home that evening. But no sooner had he taken the first sip than she said, "Taylor, I've decided to go."

"Go where?"

"Home. I've decided to move back home."

He took a sip of beer. "Why?"

"It's only a matter of time before I do anyway. I can't go on living in limbo. I want to be at home, in my own surroundings, while I'm recuperating from the miscarriage. Since I'm working out of the living room there, I might just as well consolidate everything under one roof."

One terse expletive summed up his estimation of her decision. "You're leaving because of what happened this morning, aren't you?" She glared at him stubbornly. "Aren't you?"

"All right, yes!"

Turning his back on her, he finished the beer in one long swallow. He swore beneath his breath, but loud enough for the coarse words to raise the hairs on the back of her neck. At last he came around slowly. "Are you afraid of me, Ria?"

It was such an alien concept, it took a moment for her to assimilate it. Finally she shook her head. "No, Taylor."

"I would never hurt you. You know that, don't you?"

"Yes. I told you this morning that I knew you were half-asleep and unaware of what we were doing."

"You did?"

"Yes, but I'm not sure you were listening."

He chuckled with chagrin. "When I got to work, I couldn't remember exactly what we'd said, but I was fairly certain I'd made an ass of myself."

"Never that. But you were upset. So was I."

"I wanted to be with you last night for your sake, not for mine."

"I know that."

"You don't think I was taking advantage of you?"

"No. I asked you to stay with me. I wanted you to." She clasped her hands together and wet her lips nervously. "But it appears we can't be friends, Taylor. This sexual pull between us is too strong. It puts too much strain on a friendship. If I stay here now, we'll end up fighting all the time like we did this morning. I don't want that to happen. And I don't think you do either. It would be best if I moved out tonight."

"Don't go." His voice, his eyes, were compelling. She felt herself being drawn into them as a fallen leaf is magnetically pulled into a whirlpool. "I have to, Taylor."

"Just because you lost the baby doesn't mean that I relinquish all responsibility for you. It made me mad as hell that you paid the hospital bill. I wanted to do that. It was my duty. I'm legally your husband, no matter what happens in our bed. I want to look after you until I'm certain you're physically and emotionally healed."

Ria stifled a sob and covered her face with her hands. What he was saying was beautiful, but the motivation behind his words was wrong. She would have loved for him to pamper her, but out of love, not a sense of responsibility. "I don't know what to do."

"If you stay, I swear I won't touch you. Not even a single friendly gesture." She raised her head slowly and gave him a skeptical look. "Right. Who am I kidding?" he asked himself out loud.

Miserably Ria tottered between what she wanted and what she knew was best for her. She loved him too much to stay, and she loved him too much to go. Since he was looking at her with such evident longing, how could she leave? But how could she not, knowing that every day she stayed would only make leaving more difficult?

She didn't delude herself into thinking that he loved her, or that he would eventually fall in love with her. If there had been a chance of that, he would have contacted her after Christmas Eve. Since they'd been living together, he'd had countless opportunities to profess his love. Passionate times in bed. In the quiet aftermath of lovemaking. Moments when they'd met each other's eyes across the room and a special smile was the only intimacy they'd exchanged.

He claimed to admire and respect her, to revere her for conceiving his child, and to lust for her. But he didn't love her. That he could be so ignorant of and insensitive to her love for him made her not only disconsolate, but angry.

"What do you suggest?" she asked him. "That we continue to live together, granting each other sexual favors, until it's convenient for you that I move out?"

The cutting edge of her voice was rapier-sharp, and Taylor automatically threw up a shield. "No," he replied just as harshly. "I suggest a compromise. You stay, but we'll keep it strictly platonic. No sleeping together. No nothing."

"We tried that. It didn't work."

"We'll make it work this time."

Her conviction was wavering. "One of us will have to take the couch."

"I will. It's my career we're trying to protect. I'm the one who's insisting."

"If I stay, I demand equal time on the couch."

"Look," he said crossly, "allow me to cling to chivalry and offer the lady the bed, all right?"

"Oh, all right. How long does this have to last—until you're sworn in?"

"Right. The middle of May."

"Six weeks," they said simultaneously.

Ria recovered from the coincidence first. "What happens if I get a clean bill of health before you get sworn in?"

"You tell me."

Her chin went up. "Nothing happens. The same rules apply."

"You have my word of honor." He gave her a lecherous once-over. "Do I have yours?" he drawled.

"Yes," she said, seething.

"All right, then, it's agreed. We can congratulate ourselves for approaching this in an adult, civilized manner. As soon as our obligations to each other are fulfilled, we'll separate and pursue our own interests." He stuck out his hand. "Deal?"

The terms of the agreement were rotten, but Ria shook his hand.

Eight

"What do you think?" Ria asked her husband over her shoulder.

"You're a genius."

"Can't you be more original? You told me that the night we met."

"I did?"

"Something to that effect. You said I was pretty, smart, and had a good sense of humor and my own fur coat."

"You've even got good teeth."

Smiling because he remembered as well as she did, Ria rolled up the blueprint she had been showing off and stored it in a cabinet. She'd only been in her office for two weeks. So far she'd managed to keep things tidy. Unfortunately, neatness wasn't a priority. Before long she hoped to have so much business, she wouldn't have time to keep things straight.

The set of house plans she had shown Taylor tonight was her first commission. She had demanded a hefty sum and had gotten it. The money would retard the steady dwindling of her bank account. That was one thing she had stood firm on—the segregation of the family income. Taylor had offered to help her through the transition of becoming self-employed, but she had refused to accept financial aid from him. Because their tenuous marriage was working out well in all other areas, he'd let the subject drop.

After switching out the light and locking the office door, the two of them went down the steps and got into the Corvette. "Hungry?" he asked.

He had dropped her at her office several hours earlier, and she had burned the midnight oil while he went to his health club to burn calories.

"No, just tired. I'm ready for bed."

"Yeah, me too."

They glanced at each other quickly, then away. It had been almost a month since the miscarriage, a month since Ria had agreed to live with him in a platonic relationship. They had made an effort not to rock the boat, going overboard only when it came to being polite and courteous. Each had become a model roommate. They shared cooking and cleaning duties, ideas, jokes, a *TV Guide*, toothpaste. They shared just about everything. Except a bed.

"Tough day?" Ria asked, deliberately avoiding what could have developed into a discussion of sex or the lack of it. They swapped hairbrushes, but never sexual innuendoes. References to sex were prohibited. For that very reason it was always uppermost in their minds.

"No tougher than usual. Bleeker is slinging mud about my city-council attendance record. He failed to point out that during the week he's referring to, I had the flu."

"What a sore loser."

Taylor smiled, but let the conversation lapse. By now she was sensitive to his moods, and recognized this as a reflective one. He had something disturbing on his mind. In deference to that, she didn't interrupt his thoughts with unnecessary chatter.

When they arrived home, Ria excused herself and went into the bathroom to undress. These days Taylor was sleeping in the den, on the new sleeper sofa he'd had delivered to the house. Ria had offered to take it over and give him back his bedroom, or at least to take turns sleeping in the den, but he'd been as adamant about that as she'd been about maintaining her financial independence.

Every night she went into the bedroom alone. After she came out of the bathroom, he went in. Tonight there was no break in their routine, except that when he came out of the bathroom, he didn't immediately say good night and leave the room.

Instead, dressed only in his briefs, he hesitantly moved toward the bed. Ria's mouth went dry at the sight of him. The indirect lighting cast erotic patterns of light and shadow on his body. She had often wondered if God himself had implanted each strand of Taylor's body hair. The placement of it was that perfect.

"Would you mind rubbing some of this on me?" He held out a tube of ointment.

"Sure," she said lightly, revealing none of the desire pumping through her. He handed her the tube and sat down on the edge of the bed, facing outward. "Where?"

"Do I get to choose?" Breaking their rule against innuendo, he shot her a naughty glance over his bare shoulder.

"Yes," she replied with just as naughty a wink, "but think twice before you do. This stuff is mentholated."

He winced. "In that case, you'd better make it my right shoulder."

Laughing, she squeezed a nickel-sized pool of the cream into her palm, then, kneeling behind him, applied it to his shoulder. "There?"

"A little to the . . . ah, there. Right there."

There, right there, Taylor.

You're so tight, so good.

Right there. Don't stop.

I won't.

Ria's hands were trembly as she squeezed out more of the cream. Her knees were tucked up against his firm buttocks. His skin was sleek and taut. He kept it tanned by doing yard work every Saturday, wearing nothing but cut-offs. Ria had longed to smooth her hands over those supple muscles, at which stolen glances had kept her glued to the window more than once. She indulged herself now and leaned against him, spacing her thighs so that they pressed against his back on either side of his spine. As she rubbed in the ointment, the tips of her breasts grazed him, becoming stimulated in the process.

"Did you pull a muscle?"

The massage, which should have been soothing, was having the opposite effect on him. His breathing was choppy and his muscles were contracting, not relaxing. "I must have. It was sore after my workout."

"You were pushing too hard."

Is that too hard? Am I pushing too hard?

No, no, no.

"Yeah, well, I try to exhaust myself at the gym so I don't come home wanting—"

She snatched her hands back as though his skin had burned her. Rolling her lips inward, she held them there as long as she held her breath.

Then, tentatively, she resumed rubbing the ointment in.

"Taylor?"

He cleared his throat. "Hm?"

"You could go to somebody else."

He turned his head. "What?"

She hadn't realized how hard the words would be to get out until she tried to say them. "I don't expect you to be faithful."

"How do you know I have been?"

The question stunned her, dazed her, as though he'd walloped her in the head. "I—I don't. Have you?"

"Look at me and I think you'll know the answer to that," he said with a growl.

Ria quelled the surge of happiness in her breast and tried to analyze their situation from a masculine point of view. "I'd understand if you, you know, went to another woman."

"And got laid?" Ria lowered her eyes and nodded. He swore softly. "It's not that easy."

"It used to be."

"I wasn't married then."

"You aren't married now. Not in that sense."

"But that's our little secret, isn't it?"

"I'm sure there are plenty of women who wouldn't care whether you're married or not."

"I'm sure there are too. But I care."

"Oh, of course. Because of your position in the community."

He sprang off the bed, yanking the tube of ointment from her hands. "Thanks." He stamped out of the room without looking back.

Five minutes later Ria stood in the open doorway of the den. He was on his back on the sleeper sofa, lying across it diagonally to accommodate his height. His head was resting on one hand. The other was lying on his chest. When he saw

Ria, a muscle in his cheek twitched, but he didn't move.

"May I come in?"

"What for?"

"To apologize."

He only shrugged indifferently. She had to hide her smile. He was pouting. On bare feet, she crossed the room and sat down on the edge of the mattress. It was the best sleeper sofa money could buy, but that still wasn't saying much.

"I didn't mean to make you angry."

That was like slicing through the leash of a greyhound. He was off. "I can't just go out and invite the first woman I meet into the sack, Ria. It's not that simple."

Experience would prove otherwise, but now wasn't the appropriate time to point that out.

"It's hard to cruise the clubs and pick up women when you're married and you're the mayor-elect and everybody in town knows your face," he said.

"I don't remember suggesting that you cruise. I thought you might have someone you could go to, someone who would understand our arrangement." She paused for several beats before she added, "Like Lisa."

He laughed scoffingly. "It peeved her just a little that I got married. She's not speaking to me."

Ria swallowed thickly. "You've seen her?"

"We run into each other now and then."

Why hadn't she learned a lesson from Pandora and kept the box closed on this topic? A very ugly surprise had jumped out to mock her. Apparently it had crossed Taylor's mind to take up with Lisa Burton again. It was Lisa who was unwilling.

"Well, anyway, I'm sorry for bringing it up," Ria said softly, her heart aching. "I didn't know it would upset you."

Twin blue eyes nailed her to the spot. "You've

been bringing it up for a month, and it never fails to upset me." The huskily spoken words sounded kissable. They looked kissable, lingering there on his sulky lips. "The reason I haven't gone to another woman is because I haven't wanted another woman."

Ria bowed her head and closed her eyes, willing herself not to bend over him and treat herself to a taste of his mouth. He was keeping to their agreement; she mustn't tamper with it.

When he saw that she planned to stick to her resolve, he told her good night and rudely reached for the lamp. "No, wait, Taylor. There's something else on your mind tonight, isn't there?" If she couldn't be his lover, she could be his confidante. "I was so caught up in the house plans that I didn't notice your moodiness earlier. Do you want to talk it over with me?"

"No. I wish I didn't have to mention it at all." He gazed at the ceiling for a moment. She waited him out. At last he looked at her. "We, as a couple, were invited to attend an official opening. I was told that we were the committee's unanimous choice as the guests of honor, perfect for the occasion, since we are young and newlywed."

"What did this committee invite us to open officially?"

"The new wing of the Presbyterian hospital."

Everything inside Ria shriveled up. "Oh."

"You know, then, what the new wing is for?"

"Obstetrics. Babies."

"Yeah, babies. Nurseries full of them. New fathers acting like fools and grinning like imbeciles. Grandparents taking snapshots through the window."

"Mothers with milk in their breasts," Ria said tonelessly, staring into near space.

Taylor reached up and stroked her neck. His

hand slid down into the neckline of her night-gown and covered her breast. "I'm sorry, Ria. I didn't want to tell you about it, but I was afraid you'd find out some other way."

"We're going to do it, aren't we?"

"No."

"What did you tell them?"

"I stalled them. Said that I had to check your schedule and get back to them."

"When is the grand opening?"

"The day after tomorrow. The committee didn't build in much time for us to decline gracefully," he said with a bitter laugh. "But that's just too damn bad."

"Taylor, we must do it. Even if we weren't young and newlywed, you're the mayor-elect. We're a natural to make the opening official."

Taylor shook his head adamantly. "I hated to turn them down flat, but I refuse to put you, *us*, through that, Ria."

"They don't know about the child we lost. I wasn't in that hospital. They'll think it's odd if you refuse."

"Tough. I'm a public servant, but not a slave."

"There's been so much publicity about this facility. I'm sure the opening will get a lot of media coverage. You need to be there. As your wife, I need to be there with you."

"Ria, no."

She covered his hand, which still rested against her breast. "Yes. You have to represent city hall."

"Screw city hall."

"You don't mean that."

"I do if it means you have to officiate at that damned ribbon cutting."

"It will be good therapy for me. Sort of like getting back on a horse after he's thrown you."

"You're sure?" he asked, his gaze probing.

"I'm sure."

A long silence fell between them as they stared at each other. They knew that sooner or later they'd have to acknowledge that he was still fondling her breast, but each seemed content to let it be later.

At last, speaking in a low, throbbing voice, Taylor said, "You feel very full."

"I am."

"I saw the wrappers in the wastebasket, Ria."

She had intentionally left the wrappers where he could see them. Without having to come right out and tell him, that was her way of letting him know that she was healing properly.

"Everything's okay?"

"Yes," she replied hoarsely. "And on schedule, too."

"Good."

His hand continued its gentle kneading. They became the nucleus of each other's universe. Finally, propping himself up on one elbow, Taylor kissed her, pressing his lips fervently against her breast.

When he eased back he said thickly, "You'd better go to bed now, Ria. Good night."

"Good night."

Somnambulantly, she left him.

It was like dressing for a funeral. She wanted to look her best, but she couldn't understand why it should matter. Even the first dress she had considered wearing was black. She changed her mind and selected a red one instead, but wore a wide-brimmed black straw hat with it.

Taylor did a double take when she came into the living room, where he was waiting for her, already dressed. "You look fantastic."

"Thank you. Is the hat too much?"

"It's great. And you know how partial I am to those pearls."

It just slipped out, that innocent reminder of their not-so-innocent wedding night, when Ria had met him in bed wearing only an inviting smile and her pearls.

To cover the resulting awkwardness, she turned and picked up her handbag. Taylor went in search of the car keys. They made several attempts at conversation during the trip downtown, but they were too edgy to think logically, and finally gave up trying.

When they arrived at the hospital, he reached across the console and squeezed her hand. "It's not too late to back out. We can call in sick."

"Don't be silly." In fact she did feel sick to her stomach.

"I can do this alone."

She shook her head and gave him a shaky smile. "Part of my duties as the wife of a mayor-elect. Let's go."

They made a picture-perfect couple as they were escorted into the wide marble foyer of the new obstetrics center. Ria was half a foot shorter than her husband. They were physically compatible. Both had dark hair. One had vivid blue eyes, the other vivid green. Taylor was dressed in a dark gray suit, but the fabric was lightweight enough to fit the season. Ria could have stepped out of the pages of *Vogue*. They dazzled the crowd that greeted them.

The photographers had a field day, posing them for snapshots with hospital executives and other dignitaries. Delia Starr was among the reporters covering the story. She alone knew what private agony the MacKensies must be suffering, and gave them a thumbs-up sign for encouragement.

Taylor was the public official, but Ria was handed the oversized gold scissors with which to cut the plaited pink-and-blue ribbons. When she did, everyone applauded.

"If you would indulge us, Mrs. MacKensie, Councilman, we'd like to take your picture with the first woman to give birth in the new facility."

Ria and Taylor graciously conceded. They were led down the corridor. Taylor's hand encircled Ria's elbow. "Damn, I'm proud of you. Everybody adores you. You're wonderful." He had to duck beneath the brim of her hat to whisper directly into her ear. "I know this is agony for you."

"I can't cry," she said fiercely. "But all this baby stuff . . ."

"I know. Hang in there, darling. A few more pictures and I'll get you out of here fast."

The honored mother was a woman in her early twenties, who had given birth to her first child the day before. She had prettied herself up for the photographers, and lay against the pillows of the hospital bed smiling beatifically. She blushed furiously when Taylor shook her hand, and seemed intimidated by Ria's sophistication. Her husband, who was just as young as she, stood nearby, grinning proudly.

By the time the photographers had finished, the new mother had lost her bashfulness. "Do you have kids?" she asked Ria.

"No." Ria groped for Taylor's hand. "We've only been married a couple of months."

Taylor not only clasped Ria's hand, but placed a supportive arm around her waist. "We plan to. Soon."

"I recommend it," the young woman said. She and her husband exchanged a smile. "It's great. Have you met Jennifer yet?"

"Jennifer?" Ria asked weakly.

"That's what we named our daughter."

"Uh, no, we . . . we haven't seen the nursery yet." Thank God, Ria was thinking.

But just then a member of the hospital staff wedged his way forward. "That's our next stop. Please, everybody, this way. We're going to show Councilman and Mrs. MacKensie the nursery. Technologically, it's state-of-the-art. I want you to see the neonatal nursery, too. The strides that have been taken . . ." He rambled on, flanking Ria on one side while Taylor lent support on the other.

"Excuse us just a moment," Taylor said. Halting the procession, he drew Ria aside and looked at her closely. "Let me make our excuses."

"No, you can't," she said, gripping his arm. "I'm fine."

"You're as pale as a ghost."

"Fluorescent lighting doesn't flatter my coloring."

"Don't joke with me, Ria. I want to get you out of here. Now."

"No, please."

"Is anything wrong?" the hospital administrator inquired from a discreet distance.

"No." Ria turned a brilliant smile on him. "Taylor was only asking me to remind him to send a bouquet of flowers to the new mother and Jennifer." She looked up at her husband, begging him to go along with her lie.

Their hosts breathed a collective sigh of relief. "How thoughtful," one of them murmured.

"That's one of the reasons I married him." Ria hooked her arm through Taylor's. He covered her cold, clammy fingers with his own. Only he realized that she was clutching his arm for support, and not out of affection.

They toured the neonatal nursery first, but there were no preemies there yet. When they moved toward the regular nursery, Taylor felt Ria's grip tighten on his arm. He tried to listen to the information being fed him by one of the hospital's public-relations staff, but he was concentrating so hard on Ria, he didn't digest any of the statistics.

Through the panes of glass they watched a nurse pick up a crying baby. "That's Jennifer. Our first baby," they were told.

"May I hold her?"

Ria's softly spoken request caused a hush to fall over the group of dignitaries. It even paralyzed and rendered mute the press people, who were as ill-behaved and restless as children in church. Taylor looked like he'd just swallowed an egg whole.

One of the newspaper photographers shouted, "Hey, that'd make a great shot." Several of his cohorts agreed.

The staff held a brief consultation, after which Ria was led into the nursery. Taylor felt like a prisoner's visitor, separated from his loved one by a glass wall. He could see Ria, but he couldn't touch her, couldn't alleviate her pain, and that was hell. She had prescribed this torture for herself as some kind of therapy or self-flagellation. He was powerless to help her through it.

She smiled at the nurse, then held out her arms to receive the squirming, squalling baby girl. She handled the infant far more carefully than the nurse had done, as she lowered herself into a rocking chair.

Cameras clicked and flashed around him, but Taylor wasn't aware of them. Comments and questions were batted back and forth, but he didn't hear them. His attention was focused solely on his wife, whose lovely left hand, wearing his wedding ring, supported the child's head.

"Your wife's got guts, Taylor."

Recognizing Delia Starr's voice, he nodded. "You're damn right she does," he said proudly. He remembered how delicious, yet how undaunted, Ria had looked the day she came to his office to tell him she was carrying his child. She looked just as ravishing and in complete control now, but he knew she was dying on the inside. He'd never known a woman who was as much starch as cream puff.

She gazed down into the baby's face. Taylor could tell by the way she held her lips that she was crooning to it. The baby stopped crying. Ria's smile became a soft laugh of pure delight. He couldn't hear it, but he felt it deep in his gut.

Ria addressed several comments to the nurse, but she never took her eyes off the baby. Unwrapping the pink flannel blanket, she studied the mottled limbs. She measured a foot along her thumb. She ran her finger down the child's cheek.

Before returning the baby to the nurse, she prized open one tiny fist and laid a gentle kiss in the palm.

She didn't cry until they reached home.

Taylor drove them straight there, though it wasn't even noon yet. Ria had smiled for the cameras and congratulated the hospital staff on the new facility. She'd shaken hands with everyone before they left. But on the way home she held herself ramrod-straight in the passenger's seat and didn't utter a single sound.

They went in through the front door. She set her handbag on the hall table. Taylor dropped his keys beside it. He reached for her and pulled her against him. She didn't resist.

"Hold me, please."

"You don't have to ask."

Only then did she let go her tears.

Taylor knocked her hat to the floor. He pulled out her hairpins and worked his fingers through the heavy strands as they unwound. With his fingers pressing directly against her scalp, he tucked her head beneath his chin and held her tight. The sobs hammered through her body, pounding their way up through her chest and throat. She gripped his lapels and soaked the front of his shirt with thick, heavy tears.

When her weeping subsided, he lifted her in his arms and carried her into the bedroom. He stood her beside the bed and turned her around. He unzipped her dress and pushed it down until she dutifully stepped out of it, leaving her in a satin slip with a lace top.

Treating her like a child, he turned her to face him again and placed his hands on her shoulders, applying pressure until she sat down on the edge of the bed. Kneeling, Taylor removed her high-heeled pumps and set them aside.

He left her sitting there while he took off his suit jacket, vest, and shirt. He stepped out of his shoes and peeled off his socks; then, wearing only trousers, lay on the bed and pulled Ria down with him.

She lay across his torso with her cheek resting on his breastbone. He wrapped his arms around her protectively and propped his chin on the crown of her head.

"Tell me everything about it."

"She was beautiful," Ria whispered.

"No newborn is beautiful."

She didn't take umbrage, because she knew he was teasing. "She was."

"It's amazing how small she was."

"Tiny. I don't think you could see her toes, but they were incredibly small. And her fingers, almost translucent."

He lifted Ria's hand to his mouth and kissed the backs of her fingers. "What did it feel like to touch her?"

"Her skin was very soft." Her brow puckered, remembering. "But it was dry and flaky in spots. I asked the nurse about that, and she said it was normal for newborns. They spend nine months immersed in water, so their skin is dry for a week or so after they're born, and they often peel."

"I didn't know that. What else?"

"Her heartbeat was fast. You could see it in her chest and in the soft spot on her head. Her body was warm. That's why they don't smother them with blankets. Their bodies generate much more heat than ours."

Taylor doubted that. At the moment he didn't think any human body had ever generated more heat than his. His motives were honorable, but holding Ria this way was having a profound and involuntary effect on him.

The ecru satin slip molded to every curve of her body, delineating breast, waist and hip. Her breasts lay full and lush on his chest, overflowing the stretchy lace cups of the slip. Her nipples were rosy-brown disks that one moment he longed to gaze at, and the next hoped that he wouldn't even catch a glimpse of. Each time he did, he ached to stroke, to taste.

The circuits in his mind were going haywire, trying consciously to tamp down his mounting desire and blot out what his imagination was projecting onto his brain. He could see the outline of her garter-belt suspenders beneath the clinging slip. Above the tops of her stockings he knew her thighs were smooth and soft. They formed a satiny passage to the sweet, dark mystery of her femininity.

Ria must have been alerted to his arousal. She tried to move, but he drew her back. "I ought to change and go to work," she said.

If she'd spoken with conviction, he would have

let her go. But her limp protest was his indication that she really didn't want to. "As mayor-elect, I decree that we take the rest of the day off."

"And do what?"

"This."

"What exactly is this? A wake for the baby that never was?"

"If you want to look at it that way. You're not through grieving yet."

Ria's hand covered his heart. Her thumbnail mindlessly raked his nipple. "Am I being ridiculously self-centered, Taylor? Thousands of women each day, all over the world, suffer miscarriages."

"Each one feels exactly the way you do, if she cares anything about the child."

"And if she cares for the man who fathered it." She lifted her head and looked down into his face. "Most men in your situation would have been relieved when I lost the baby."

"Never that, Ria."

"It got you off the hook."

"I didn't feel hooked. I wanted the baby too."

Tears welled up in her eyes again. She caught her lower lip between her teeth. "You did, didn't you?"

"Very much."

"I wonder if it was a boy, or a little girl like Jennifer."

"Don't."

"Did we lose a prima ballerina or an Olympic gold medalist, a statesman or scientist or artist?"

"Don't, don't." He rolled her to her back and levered himself above her. "We'll go crazy if we think about that." He sipped the tears off her cheeks and lips. "And I'll go crazy if I don't kiss you."

At first it was a gentle kiss. His lips merely settled against hers. They breathed each other's breath. Then his lips parted and took hers in a possessive, wanting kiss. His tongue was bold and invasive and made rapacious love to her mouth.

She threaded her fingers up through his hair. "Taylor, Taylor"—she groaned—"kiss me until it doesn't hurt anymore."

"Where do you hurt?"

"Everywhere."

He covered her tear-streaked cheeks with random kisses, returning again and again to her mouth. He worked the straps of her slip down her shoulders and buried his face in the fragrant velvet softness of her cleavage. He kissed her breasts, pressing his lips firmly into the giving flesh, then tongue-massaging her nipples to stiff peaks.

He nuzzled her delta through the warm satin that slid over her flesh as though caressing it. Lifting the slip's fluted hem, he burrowed his face in the cushion of her belly, kissed her navel lightly, airily, then probed it aggressively with his tongue.

"Oh, Taylor, stop. I'm getting—"

"What?"

'Wet."

"Good."

"But what good will it do to go so far and—"

He pushed his hand into her panties and between her thighs. "Ride with it."

She demurred. Seductively he ground the heel of his hand against her. Craving freedom from the ribbons of desire his kisses had bound her in, Ria followed his whispered instructions.

And when the waves of release washed through her sex, his lips were there to catch them, sighing endearments.

Minutes later, her body still aglow and tingling, her breath still uneven, Ria felt Taylor ease himself off the bed. She opened her eyes and spoke his name lovingly.

"I'm not going far." He leaned over her and brushed damp strands of hair off her shoulders and chest. "I'll be right back."

Shaking her head, Ria sat up and inched to the edge of the bed. She slid her arms around his narrow waist and rested her cheek against his bare stomach before kissing it. And again, more wantonly, using her tongue.

"Ria," he rasped out.

Then she seductively unbuckled his belt.

Nine

Ria pressed her foot hard against the emergency brake and pushed open the car door. As she got out, her handbag slid to the driveway, and everything spilled out. Muttering unladylike swear words, she scooped it all up and hurriedly let herself in the back door.

The telephone was ringing. "Hello?"

"Hi," Taylor said. "You sound breathless."

"I just came in."

"I thought you'd be here by now."

"I thought so too. But I got held up." She was supposed to have been at his office fifteen minutes before. He might be irritated with her now, but he wouldn't be when he learned where she'd been and why she was running late. "It'll only take me half an hour to change."

"That'll put us late getting there, Ria."

She thought for a moment. "You go on and I'll meet you there."

"I hate to, but maybe I should."

"They can't start without you, and they'll be

frantic if you're late. I'll catch up with you at the hotel."

"There's a predinner cocktail reception. I'm not sure which suite it's in."

"This is one night you can't possibly get lost. Don't worry. I'll find you."

"If you have any trouble—"

"I won't. Now, say good-bye. I don't want to make you late."

"Okay, 'bye. Oh, Ria, what held you up? Work?"

"I'll tell you when I get there."

She hung up before he could say any more. Tonight was the big night. Taylor MacKensie was being sworn in as mayor, following a formal banquet in the ballroom of one of the city's major hotels.

Ria raced into the bedroom, kicking off her shoes and shrugging off her suit jacket as she went. Usually neat to a fault, she dropped clothes as she shed them on her way to the shower. The water was hot and invigorating.

But it couldn't compare to the effervescence that was bubbling inside her. She'd seen her doctor that afternoon. Knowing she was going to be cutting it close to get to the banquet on time, it had been annoying to arrive for her appointment, only to learn the doctor's schedule was backed up due to an emergency that morning. She'd gone through every *National Geographic* twice and had read much more about wildebeests than she wanted to know, before she'd finally been summoned into the examination room.

But what the doctor had to tell her had been worth the long wait and all the frustration. She was fit as a fiddle. There was no reason why she couldn't resume marital relations.

Ria's hands trembled now as she poked earrings into her ears. Tonight when they got home she would tell Taylor the good news. Thinking about what would inevitably follow made her giddy. Since the afternoon of their "wake," they'd been like drops of water on a hot skillet. They sizzled.

For that reason they'd cautiously avoided touching each other. He hadn't begun sleeping with her again, as she had expected, and secretly hoped, that he would. That night, and every night since, he'd stayed in the den on the sleeper sofa.

She had tried to figure out what had made their lovemaking that afternoon so different. It had been as passionate as ever, but there had been another quality added. An intensity. They had entered into a dimension of sexuality where giving superceded receiving. It had frightened them, this emotion behind their passion.

They worked at keeping the mood in the house light and friendly, while beneath the surface it teemed with suppressed longing and unspoken feelings. They couldn't last much longer without cracking under the pressure. Now they wouldn't have to.

Ria felt certain that once they resolved their sexual relationship, the subject of an annulment would be tabled for good.

The evening was cool enough for her to wear the sequin dress she had worn on Christmas Eve. She misted herself with the perfume Taylor liked best, put a Kleenex and a lipstick in her silver handbag, snatched up her car keys, and left by way of the back door.

She could swear that her feet weren't touching the ground.

Most of those who had attended the predinner reception had already migrated from the suite to the ballroom several floors below. Taylor excused himself to use the rest room. When he came out, only one other person remained in the suite—Lisa.

Looking sensational in a slinky black dress that set off her blond hair, she smiled at him from the wet bar. "Refill?"

"No, thanks, I've got to hurry and get downstairs."

"Can you spare me a minute, Taylor? We've hardly spoken to each other in weeks."

"You seemed to want it that way."

She stirred her fresh drink with her fingertip, then sucked it clean. "Do you blame me for being upset when you went behind my back and married that Lavender woman?"

His lips narrowed in irritation. "Her name is Ria. And blame is too strong a word. Surprised would be more like it. I'm surprised that you've been upset over my marriage. We were always free to see other people."

"See, but not marry."

Taylor was enough of a politician to recognize a Mexican standoff. Instinctually he knew when to retreat. "Excuse me." He headed toward the door.

"Taylor, I'm sorry." Lisa reached for his arm as he brushed past her. "I thought we had an understanding."

"We did. The understanding was that there was no understanding."

She gazed up at him through her lashes. "I didn't realize how much you meant to me until I lost you. I've missed you."

"Have you?"

She set her drink down and pressed herself against him, looping her arms around his neck. He felt her pert, braless breasts against his chest. "Very much. And I know you've missed me."

"How do you know that?"

Her smile was as smug as a reader who guessed who done it after skimming only one chapter of an Agatha Christie. "What you and your wife do in bed couldn't be as good as what we did."

"It's different," he said diplomatically.

She cuddled him between her slightly parted thighs and felt him grow hard behind the fly of his tuxedo trousers. "Keep your wife, Taylor," she whispered. "I had a husband and discovered that marriage wasn't for me. I like being unencumbered. But I also like you. A lot." She rubbed against him like a she-cat in heat. "We're both discreet. I see no reason why we can't continue as before. Before you got careless and knocked up Ria Lavender."

His eyes turned cold as he said curtly, "Ria's not pregnant."

Lisa smiled maliciously. "Not now. But she was. That's why you married her, isn't it? When did it happen, Christmas Eve, after the Grahams' party?" Her eyes narrowed. "I envision this scenario. You were angry with me for going on the ski trip without you. You met a reasonably attractive woman at the party. She had no scruples about a one-night stand. You went to bed together.

"Ah, well, I forgive you, darling. You're a man. I know better than anyone how virile you are. Besides," she added mischievously, "I was snuggled up with a ski instructor at the time."

She puckered her lips and made a *tsk*-ing sound. "I walked away from that rowdy encounter unscathed. Isn't it a shame that you got caught? Poor baby, you did the honorable thing and married the girl. For nothing."

Taylor had more common sense than to nibble at Lisa's bait. He would admit nothing. Nor would he argue points just to set the record straight. Oddly enough, her sordid capsulization was enlightening. Was that how Ria felt? Did she still feel like nothing more than a receptacle for his lust?

Goda'mighty, until now, he'd never looked at this thing from her point of view. He needed to clarify things. Soon. He couldn't let her go on thinking that she had been, and still was, nothing but a convenient roll in the hay.

But first he had to deal with Lisa. He feigned boredom. "You don't know what you're talking about, Lisa."

She tossed her head back and laughed. "Oh, but I do. Delia Starr likes to drink, Taylor. Remember that the next time you grant her an interview. After a few Scotches, her tongue unwinds like a spool of thread, and she tells all."

"What do you intend to do with this information? Blackmail me? What's the price of keeping you quiet, sexual favors? Do I have to play stud for you to shut you up?"

"I'd never stoop to anything so crass." She slipped her hands into his coat and tweaked his nipples through his shirt. "But people are interested in their new mayor and his bride. I might blurt out something in conversation that I didn't intend to."

"You're a slut."

She flinched, but recovered quickly and smiled lazily. "You're right. But I've got a lot of money. I move in the right social and political circles. You can't afford to make me unhappy." She stretched up and kissed him softly. "What's the problem, Taylor? I'm not asking that you give up your wife. I don't object to her as long as she doesn't interfere with us. A brunette wife and a blond mistress. What more could a man ask for?"

She breathed the question against his lips, then came up on tiptoe and arched herself against him. He grabbed her around the waist to maintain his balance. Lisa's open mouth moved carnivorously over his; her tongue darted in and around his lips.

It was a sudden intake of breath that caused Taylor to whip his head around. Ria was standing in the doorway. She was a glittering, dazzling sight in the sequin dress. Her glossy black hair shone just as brightly as the dress, and her eyes reflected the same light.

But they were icy.

Taylor pushed Lisa away. "Ria."

"Good evening, Mrs. MacKensie," Lisa said, laughing.

"Good evening," Ria replied coolly. She moved her gaze from the woman to her husband. "They told me downstairs I could find you here."

"Ria, this isn't what it looks like."

"Taylor, how trite," she said. "I hope you're more eloquent when you give your acceptance speech." Turning on her heel, she left the room. Taylor knocked Lisa aside on his lunging, headlong pursuit of his wife, who was halfway down the corridor by the time he caught up with her.

"Ria, wait a minute."

"We haven't got a minute. We're going to be late for the banquet."

"You're staying?"

"That was our agreement, wasn't it?" she asked tightly. "That I remain with you until you were officially sworn in? I'm going to sit beside you at the head table and smile and pretend that I didn't just catch you slobbering all over your whore."

She angrily punched the elevator button. The doors opened immediately, and she stepped inside. He got in with her, but she didn't give him time to speak. "You're jumping the gun, aren't you? When you said we'd pursue our own interests, it was my understanding that you meant *after* tonight. Obviously I was wrong."

"You refuse to listen to an explanation, don't you?" Taylor asked as they rode down.

She smiled up at him sweetly. "Go straight to hell."

"I didn't think so," he said out of the side of his mouth. The elevator doors were already opening, and as they alighted they were surrounded by a crowd of people wanting to shake hands with the couple of the hour.

As soon as they were seated at the head table, the banquet commenced. Ria couldn't swallow a bite. She was nauseated. Her head was throbbing. Her eyes seemed determined to tear, though she willed them not to.

She couldn't concentrate on anything. Her mind was focused on Taylor holding Lisa in his arms, kissing her. She wanted to scream and shout and throw something, but she behaved impeccably, just as the first lady of the city should.

She considered excusing herself and giving sudden illness as the reason, but she was determined not to give Lisa the satisfaction of seeing her cowed. Nor would she let Taylor off that lightly. If sitting through this banquet, with its endless number of mediocre courses, was uncomfortable for her, it must have been pure hell for him. What a tight squeeze, to be wedged between one's wife and one's mistress at a dinner where one is on public display. Talk about a hot seat. Ria hoped he was frying.

The dinner was finally over. Waiters cleared the tables. People in the audience turned their chairs away from their tables in order to face the dais, where the emcee was telling jokes as stale as Ria's smile.

Following the emcee's warm-up, brief speeches

were given by various dignitaries. All of them led up to the introduction of the distinguished new mayor, Taylor MacKensie.

"And now," the emcee intoned, "I'm going to ask Taylor MacKensie and his beautiful wife, Ria, to join me at the podium for the swearing in."

Ria was stunned. She hadn't known she would be called upon to stand with him. Taylor placed his hand beneath her elbow and assisted her up. The audience applauded them as they made their way down the row of chairs next to the head table, toward the podium.

Later she didn't know how she survived those next few minutes while Taylor took his oath of office. His voice was clear and distinct. She recalled hearing it filled with humor, with fury, with passion. It seemed to seep into her marrow like a powerful narcotic. It lulled her into believing that he was a man of integrity, a man who could be trusted. A man who could be faithful to his wife. But she knew better.

After being sworn in, he smiled at the applauding audience, then turned his head and smiled down at Ria. Cupping her face, he bent his head and kissed her quickly. The ovation swelled, making the crystal cylinders vibrate in the chandeliers overhead. When he released her, the emcee escorted her back to her chair and Taylor took over the microphone. His speech was eloquent and entertaining. His confident voice rang with enthusiasm and optimism, which were contagious. When he concluded, the audience as one came to its feet.

Reluctantly Ria stood up with them to applaud her cheating husband.

After that it was only a matter of surviving another round of picture-taking and hand-shaking before they could leave. They waited together in the garage for the valet to bring their cars around. Hers arrived first. She got in and drove off, leaving him impatiently waiting for his car.

Ria was almost too upset to drive. She kept forgetting the most fundamental aspects of operating an automobile and negotiating traffic. She wanted to go to her house, but remembered that she didn't have the key with her. She'd have to go to Taylor's first. She left her car idling as she ran up the steps and unlocked the front door. A mad search through the house finally produced her other set of house keys. She was on her way back out the front door when Taylor materialized and blocked her path.

"Get out of my way, Taylor."

"No."

"I don't want to listen to anything you have to say and I know you don't want to hear what I have to say, so please, let's make this as easy on each other as possible."

"What is it that you know I don't want to hear?"

She glared up at him. "What a despicable, two-faced, hypocritical bastard you are."

"Why do you think so?"

Stunned, she fell back a step. "Maybe in your rule book it's okay for a husband to go around kissing his former bed warmer, but it's against my beliefs."

"I wasn't kissing Lisa."

"Then that was one helluva realistic dream I was having." She tried to move him aside, but he wouldn't be budged. He turned the tables on her and bodily moved her out of the way so he could close the front door. She looked up at him mutinously. "You're being childish, Taylor. I'm not staying here with you a minute longer. Why don't you stop playing bully and just let me leave?"

"Not until you know the facts."

"I witnessed the facts," she shouted. "You were either kissing fervently or one of you was giving the other mouth-to-mouth resuscitation. And if that's the case, was it necessary for her to massage your heart as well?"

The memory of Lisa's hands crawling over his chest inside his tuxedo jacket made her livid. "How could you? You were lucky that I was the one who walked in on you. My God, anybody could have seen the two of you together. Everything you've worked for would have been destroyed. Was that kiss worth it? What were you thinking of?"

"You."

She stared at him incredulously. His cruel teasing made her so angry that tears spurted from her eyes. "Damn you, don't play games with me. I don't deserve it."

"You deserve to be turned over my knee and paddled for jumping to the wrong conclusion."

"What? You were caught red-handed with your ex-lover. But then"—she snickered mirthlessly—"Lisa isn't your *ex*, is she? Has it been going on behind my naive back from the beginning? Or did you resume more recently? After the miscarriage, when I was out of commission?"

A muscle in his jaw flexed. "You'd better stop before you say something ugly that you'll regret."

"I won't regret any ugly thing I say to you. I can't even think of enough ugly things to say to you." She turned her back, wishing that the dress didn't dip so low. She felt exposed, vulnerable. "I was a fool to come to you in the first place. Then to let you talk me into staying!"

She spun around. "That's it, isn't it? Having a wife gives you respectability. It keeps your critics at bay. The baby would have been an added bonus. You probably counted yourself lucky that day I came into your office and told you I was pregnant. You saw a way to have your cake and eat it, too, didn't you? I'm a screen, shielding you while you carry on your tawdry little affairs. Well, not any longer, Taylor. I stayed with you out of a sense of duty and obligation, but no more. I've had it with you. *Finis.* This charade is over as of now."

Her breasts were heaving with agitation. Her green eyes were glittering like emeralds. At her sides, her hands were balled into fists. Every hair on her head was bristling with righteous indignation. She was quivering, as taut as a piano wire.

Rightly, he should have tucked in his tail and skulked off to nurse the wounds her tongue-lashing had inflicted. Instead he calmly asked, "Are you finished?"

"I just said as much."

"I meant with your temper tantrum, not our relationship."

"The answer to both is yes."

"Good. Now, shut up and listen to me." He pointed a finger at her. "About half of what you said is tripe." She opened her mouth to protest, but his eyes shot her a clear warning to keep quiet. "All that about your staying here out of a sense of duty and my wanting you to stay to cover my ass, that's crap. You stayed because you wanted to. I asked you to stay because I wanted you to. So let's not deceive ourselves into thinking that either one of us had an altruistic motive."

"All right, so we're both at fault for this bizarre marriage. But at least I was faithful to it."

"So was I!"

"I didn't go out and have a fling."

"Neither did I. Tonight was the first time I've even had a private conversation with Lisa since well before Christmas."

"Well, you certainly made up for lost time." Ria turned her back on him again.

This time he came up behind her, grabbed her arm, and spun her around. "I didn't even kiss her," he said through clenched teeth. "She kissed me."

"What's the difference?"

"A helluva lot."

"Your arms were around her."

"She knocked me off balance about half a second before you walked in."

"Do you expect me to believe that?"

"It's the truth."

"And I suppose you have a perfectly good explanation for why her hands were inside your coat."

"Yes. She was fondling me. But I didn't have my hands inside her dress, fondling her."

"Yet."

He swore viciously. "She stayed behind after everybody had left. She came on to me, Ria, not the other way around."

"Good thing I didn't catch you in bed together. You would have tried to convince me that she was raping you."

"Augh," he growled, raising his fists toward the ceiling.

"If you're so innocent, why did you stay in there with her?" Ria asked. "Why didn't you just walk out?"

"Because of what she was saying."

"Dirty talk? I never knew you were into that?"

The scathing look he gave her should have reduced her to a puddle of ectoplasm. "Apparently she got Delia Starr drunk. Lisa knew about our baby and the miscarriage."

He quoted his and Lisa's conversation word for word. Ria crossed her arms over her middle. It seemed profane for Lisa to know about the child she'd lost.

"So you heard her out to save your skin."

"And yours."

Ria laughed. "I guess you got aroused just to be convincing."

His face went blank with guilt. "How do you know I was aroused?"

"I can see, Taylor," she said, pointing to her eyes. "When you turned around, you were definitely . . ." She faltered, then gathered steam and shouted at him, "Aroused!"

He took two menacing steps, grabbed her hand, and plunged it down past his waist. "Yes, I was hard."

"Stop it."

"I still am. And do you know why?"

"I don't—"

"Not because of Lisa. Because of you. *You.* She was talking about you, my brunette wife. She said that what we did in bed must be good." He wouldn't release her hand, but kept it pressed against his lower body. "After she said that, it was all I could think about, us in bed."

"I don't believe you."

He knotted the fingers on his free hand in her hair and pulled her head back. His breath struck her face in hot, rapid pants. "Yes, you do. I've been hot for you since the first time I laid eyes on you. That toothpick of yours poleaxed me on Christmas Eve. I've never known desire that potent. It's still there, Ria, stronger than ever, and you damned well know it.

"In my own house I've been unable to eat or sleep or do anything else for wanting you, and trying to hide it so you wouldn't get scared off. I've tossed and turned on that blasted sleeper sofa, thinking about you in my bed, wanting to be in it with you. Beside you. Inside you. Wanting to be so deep inside you that I thought I'd go nuts if I couldn't be."

He kissed her hard and angrily, working her lips open with his. "You know I've been faithful to this marriage, Ria. Damn you, you know I have. Now, kiss me."

Anger, it seemed, had always been an aphrodisiac for them. It was frequently the spark that ignited their short fuses. Ria became pliant against him. Her neck relaxed and her head fell back, making it easy for his tongue to penetrate her lips and stroke her mouth.

She clutched the black satin lapels of his jacket, thrusting her breasts high against his chest. He bent his head and kissed her throat, working his mouth down into the deep V of her bodice.

"I want you. Oh, Lord, how I want you."

"Today . . . the reason I was late . . . I had a doctor's appointment." Taylor's head snapped up. His eyes shone like twin blue flames. "Take me to bed," Ria said huskily.

He didn't waste a second, but carried her through the darkened house into the bedroom. One small beam of light shone down from the ceiling onto the bed, making it an oasis of sensuality in the surrounding dark.

They undressed each other. Long kisses detained them, but they eventually faced each other naked. His hands moved over her, lightly, deftly. She leaned forward and took a love bite out of the meaty part of his chest and moved her hand caressingly down his middle.

They didn't bother with folding down the bed-clothes. They lay directly on top of the mink. When he parted her thighs and caressed her, she was already moist, but he kept dipping his fingers inside her until she was slippery and almost incoherent with need.

He entered her with one smooth stroke and lay motionless for a long while, relishing the way her body tightly enveloped his.

"Am I hurting you?"

"No."

He buried his face in her neck. "For the last two weeks, ever since that morning at the hospital, I've been dying to be this way with you."

"I know. Me too. I couldn't wait to tell you that we could make love again."

He kissed her mouth. Then her breasts. He began to move. Faster.

Moments later, as he lay spent beside her, he said, "Ria, there's nothing between Lisa and me. Nothing."

"I know."

"You know? Then why'd you run me through that wringer?"

She rubbed her cheek against his. "I thought I'd die when I saw you in each other's arms. I didn't really think you were betraying your wedding vows, but I wanted to be sure."

"Aren't you the one who suggested to me just a couple of weeks ago that I take a lover?"

"Yes, but I didn't mean it," she said with chagrin. "When I saw you with Lisa I was hurt, furious, jealous."

"You were jealous?"

"Well, how would you have felt if you'd caught me with Guy?"

"Jealous. Gut-sick. Murderous. I feel that way every time I think of him touching you."

"He never did."

He gazed down at her, bewildered. "What?"

"Guy couldn't have been the father of my baby even if he hadn't had a vasectomy." She laid her hand against his cheek. "I never slept with him, Taylor."

He breathed a curse, or a prayer. Then he kissed her with such tenderness, it made her weepy with love. Staring down into her eyes, he stroked her cheek. "You're the most fascinating woman I've ever met. Feminine, yet strong. Opinionated, but tactful. Ladylike, but sexy. Exasperating and exquisite. You can make me madder and get me harder than any woman I've ever known."

She laughed. "Thank you."

With his fingertip, he traced a circle around her pouting nipple. "Did I rush you?"

She lowered her eyes. "I'm not complaining."

"I'm sorry. It's just that I'd wanted you for so long, I couldn't hold back."

"I forgive you," she whispered, drawing him closer, "so long as you keep trying until you get it right."

Ten

He drove her to work the next morning and followed her into her office. No sooner had the door closed behind them than he pulled her into his arms and kissed her.

"You taste so much better than ham and eggs. I think I'll just make you my breakfast every morning from now on."

Her knees felt weak, just as they had the night before when he had kissed the backs of them. "Thanks for the ride."

"My pleasure." He ran his hands over her derriere. "What time will you be here to pick me up?"

"Five-thirtyish."

"I'll be ready."

"Hm, so will I." The double meaning was all too clear. For emphasis he kissed her with voluptuous thoroughness. When he turned to go, he caught a glimpse of her face. "Ria? Are you crying?"

"Crying? Of course not. Don't be silly."

"I thought I saw tears in your eyes."

"The sunlight. It's making my eyes water." She

went to the window and adjusted the blinds so that the sunlight coming in wasn't so direct.

Taylor took her by the shoulders and turned her around. "Are you sure there's nothing wrong? Come to think of it, you've been awfully quiet this morning."

"You haven't given me much opportunity to talk. We've been kissing ever since we woke up."

He smiled with devastating sexiness. "I can't think of a better way to spend the morning." Seductively he stroked her lips with his thumb. She turned her head away. His hand fell to his side.

"All right, let's have it."

Something about the way he hooked his thumbs in his vest pockets and assumed that arrogant stance set her teeth on edge. He was annoyed because she wasn't curling up and purring when he petted her. What was she, a trained cat? "Don't use that condescending tone of voice with me, Taylor."

"Frankly, I don't know what tone of voice to use with you. We just spent an amazing night together. It should go down in the annals of eroticism, if there is such a thing. This morning I feel like I could pole-vault Mount Everest, and you're about as cheerful as a gravedigger. What gives with you? Doesn't anything make you happy, make you feel good?

"Yes, when we're in bed together I feel great."

"So what's the problem?"

"We can't spend our lives in bed, Taylor."

"I wouldn't mind." He smiled lecherously, and his blue eyes twinkled. But when he sensed her irritation, he sobered instantly. "Sorry. I didn't mean to joke."

"Yes, you did. And rightly so. This marriage is a joke."

"Then why aren't you smiling?"

"Why didn't you call me?" she asked abruptly.

"Huh? When? Call you? What are you talking about?"

"After Christmas Eve."

"Christmas Eve?" he echoed, flabbergasted.

"Yes, Christmas Eve. Remember?"

"Yeah, I remember. It was terrific."

"Terrific sex."

"Don't say it like that. It was terrific everything. There were plenty of sparks flying before we ever lay down on that couch."

"Then why didn't you ask me out again?" He turned his back to stare out the window. Ria was crushed. She had put him on the spot. He didn't want to talk about this, and she would do well to leave the subject alone. But she couldn't. Like a sore tooth, she had to go back to it, probe it. She had to know. "Did you forget about it as soon as it was over?"

He turned around. "No. Hell, no. I thought about it. I thought about you. You were all I thought about for weeks."

Vastly relieved, she sat down on the arm of her office sofa. Softly she said, "As far as I know my phone wasn't out of order."

One corner of his mouth lifted in a smile. "I wanted to call you, Ria. Of course I did, but I couldn't bring myself to."

"Why?"

"For one thing, I was embarrassed." Her lips parted in surprise. "Yeah, embarrassed."

"But you told me that you'd had one-night stands before."

He ran a hand through his hair. "I have. Not in a long time, though. I'm more discriminating now than I was fifteen years ago." His eyes flickered back to her. "I've had casual, short-term affairs, but until last Christmas Eve I'd never been swept up so completely. What happened between us was so . . . *chemical* I couldn't put a name to it. It scared the hell out of me. I didn't want to apologize for it, and I couldn't tell you how I felt about it, because I didn't know, so it seemed better just to ignore it."

"I see."

"No, I don't think you do." He sat down on the opposite armrest. "My first impression of you was that you were gorgeous. Articulate. Fun. You seemed to have everything in your life right where you wanted it. Nothing was out of sync. You were enjoying phenomenal success in your career. There was Guy, although at the time I didn't know what a drip my competition was. I pictured the man you were seeing as having Mel Gibson's face, Bruce Jenner's body, and Sam Shepard's intellect."

She laughed. "It's funny now, but it wasn't then," he said sincerely. "There didn't seem to be a single vacancy in your life that I could fill. You put out no distress signals. You came across as a really put-together lady. I guess I was scared of being rejected if I called you."

Ria assimilated everything that he'd said, but it still didn't hang right, like a drape with one hook missing. "You were angry when I first told you about the baby, Taylor. Why?"

"Because it had taken that to get us together again. When you first called my secretary and asked for an appointment, I couldn't believe my good fortune. I got myself all worked up for an invitation to dinner. Instead you were strictly business, and about as approachable as a porcupine."

"That was a defense mechanism."

"I didn't know that then." He stood up and

moved toward her. Cradling her face between his hands, he asked, "Why didn't you ask me to stay on Christmas morning, Ria?"

"For the same reasons you didn't call me," she said huskily. "I was embarrassed, ashamed of myself, actually. I had never had a one-night-stand. I knew you were seeing another woman regularly. And remember, I woke up to find you tiptoeing out. I thought that you had gotten what you came for and were making a quick getaway to spare yourself a scene."

He bent down and kissed her softly. "No, Ria. If you had invited me to stay for breakfast, I never would have left."

She gazed up at him with perplexity. "Truly?"

He nodded. "It seems that we wasted a lot of precious time being cautious, doesn't it?" He straightened up and consulted his wristwatch. "Speaking of time, I've got a meeting with the city council to go over the budget in fifteen minutes."

"Then you'd better hurry." She walked him to the door. "This is your first day in office. You mustn't be late."

"Sure everything is okay?"

She aimed her finger at the door. "Go!" He kissed her swiftly before he left. Ria closed the door behind him, pressing her forehead against the cool wood. A tear rolled down her cheek. "Damn." She wiped it away impatiently. "What's the matter with me?"

Figuratively, she rolled up her shirt sleeves and went to work. But she found that she couldn't concentrate on the house plans spread out on her drawing board. Her mind was on her marriage. Taylor seemed to take for granted that everything was hunky-dory. And it was. They were compatible. Their sex life was incredible.

So why was she depressed?

Because she had wanted him to tell her that he loved her and he hadn't. It was that simple.

Maybe he was just one of those men who couldn't love.

But she was a woman to whom love was essential.

The Lavenders had demonstrated to an unwanted child that the miracle of love could reshape a person's destiny. It was therefore vital to Ria's existence.

No matter how thrilling every other aspect of her marriage to Taylor was, love was the missing, essential ingredient. Without it the recipe, no matter how tasty, just didn't work.

They had gone out to dinner and a movie. It was getting late and Taylor was driving slowly. His tuneless humming to the music on the radio was grating on her nerves. Her spirits were as bedraggled as laundry left on a clothesline during a heavy rain. All day she'd conducted a silent debate about what she should do.

The conclusion she had reached was to leave Taylor before her unreciprocated love for him ate her alive. What she hadn't resolved was the best way to go about it.

"Where are you going?" she asked.

"You said there were some things you wanted to pick up at your house. I thought now was a good time."

"Oh. Thanks."

"I've been thinking about this 'your house' and 'my house' business. What do we need two houses for? You were going to add on to yours. Why don't you convert those plans so they can be used for mine? We could add on to it, couldn't we? If you like it, that is."

"It's a beautiful house," she said unenthusiastically.

"Or we could sell them both and buy another one, a larger one. What do you think?"

"I don't know, Taylor." Wearily she put her elbow in the open window and rested her head in her palm. She was worried about how she was going to hold body and soul together when she left him and he was talking about houses. She'd live in a pup tent with him if he'd say he loved her.

"Well, think about it."

"Okay."

He went back to humming along with the radio. When she turned up the volume in a none-too-subtle hint for him to stop, he asked, "Something wrong?"

"You still can't sing."

"I wasn't singing. I was humming."

"You can't hum either."

"Ouch. Still sulky?"

"I'm not sulky," she said testily.

"Could have fooled me. Are you mad because I didn't call you today?"

"No, I don't expect that kind of constant attention from you."

"Why not? I'm your husband, aren't I?"

Her throat constricted with emotion. "Yes, you're my husband."

"Don't most husbands call their wives at some point during the day just to say hello and ask if they want them to pick up bread and milk on the way home?"

"Only on 'Leave it to Beaver.' "

"I'm sorry I didn't call and check in. I was very busy today. Had a million errands to run. Things to do. By the way, I stopped at the bank and deposited some money into your checking account. You were getting low."

She jerked her head around. "How do you know how much money is in my checking account?"

"I looked at the balance in your checkbook. Why are you getting so riled? I put money in; I didn't take any out."

"I just wish you had consulted me first."

"Ah, then maybe I'd better tell you that I took out life-insurance policies on both of us, naming us each other's beneficiaries."

She stared at him speechlessly. He was digging her in deeper when she was trying to find a graceful way to get out of this marriage.

But before she could say anything, the Corvette took the corner at an indiscreet speed. As soon as she righted herself, she saw the lights.

"What in the world?"

The roof of her house had been outlined in Christmas lights. The front door was framed in multicolored mini-lights, and a holly wreath with bright red bows was hanging in the center of it.

"Didn't you take down your Christmas decorations?" he asked, wheeling into the driveway.

"You know I did. What's going on? Who did this?" She didn't wait for him to open the car door, but sprang out under her own power and ran up the steps to the front door. It wasn't even locked. She went in.

Despite the warm spring night, a fire was crackling in the fireplace. The mantel had been strung with an evergreen garland, and above it, tall red candles stood like soldiers at attention. They were burning, emanating a bayberry scent. A fully decorated Christmas tree, complete with gift-wrapped presents underneath, stood in the corner where the windows met. It was a freshly cut pine. The pungent fragrance filled the room.

Mouth agape, Ria whispered, "I don't believe this. Who—"

Her eyes lighted on her silver-fox coat, which was supposed to be in storage for the summer. Instead it was spread out on the sofa. Warm color rose in her cheeks. She turned around slowly. Taylor was lounging against the doorjamb. His expression was serious, but his eyes were luminous.

"What you don't believe," he said softly, "is that I love you. I do, Ria." He gently closed the front door. Then, walking slowly, he came toward her and placed his arms around her waist.

"*You* did all this?"

"I told you I'd been very busy today."

"But—"

"Why didn't I just tell you I loved you this morning, when you were fishing so subtly? Because you would have thought I was only telling you what you wanted to hear. I thought that if I showed you rather than just told you, you'd be better convinced. Besides, I have a sentimental streak too. I think Christmas represents the ultimate demonstration of love. The idea took hold, and once it did, I didn't want to spoil the surprise."

She raised her hand to his cheek. Then, repeating his name, stretched up to kiss him. "It was killing me to live with you, make love with you, when I thought it was all one-sided. The deadline for us to stay together passed yesterday. You hadn't said anything about it."

"I was pretending that there was no deadline."

"I had decided to leave you."

"That was what I was afraid of. Not that I'd have let you go. If you'd tried, we'd have had a helluva fight, followed by a helluvan orgy, and you'd have gone on believing that all we have going for us is great sex."

"And it's not?"

"What, great? It's mind-boggling."

"No," she said, laughing when he yanked her close and snarled into her ear. "Is sex all we've got going for us?"

"Hardly." He gazed down at her and smoothed back her hair. "Our baby brought us together in the first place. Losing it could have finished us, but it didn't. The miscarriage bound us closer together. Until then I didn't really know how much I loved you. Ironically, it was when I couldn't have you sexually that I really began loving you and thinking of you as my wife."

He drew her face up to his and kissed her sweetly. Then, wrapping her in his arms, he kissed her with passion. "I love you, Ria," he breathed as they pulled apart.

"I love you too. Oh, Lord, so much. It broke my heart when you left me Christmas morning."

"It broke my heart to leave you. This time I'll stay. We'll give it another run-through tonight."

"On the sofa? On the fur?"

"Naked. You wearing nothing but firelight and a dreamy expression."

"You warm and hard."

"You soft and wet."

He moved his hands to her breasts; then his lips caressed them through her blouse. Making a yearning sound, she arched her body against his.

"Hm, sweet," he said. "But before we get to that, you missed the best part."

"I doubt that," she said, stroking the hard ridge behind his fly.

"Will you behave?"

"Why should I?"

He nodded toward the far corner.

Turning around, Ria clapped her hands together and laughed with delight. "Oh, how could I have missed that?"

More miraculous than all the other Christmas paraphernalia was a Nativity scene. There was a wooden stable with a thatched straw roof, and mannequins dressed in period clothes, representing all the principals: Mary, Joseph, the shepherds, the Wise Men. There were three life-sized woolly lambs. There was even a manger with a doll lying in it to represent baby Jesus.

It certainly was a lifelike doll. It moved. And as Ria watched in fascination, it opened its mouth and let out a howl that was definitely human and out of character for anything divine. It was a loud, lusty wail that demanded immediate gratification.

"Translated, I think that means, 'I've been quiet long enough. Feed me,'" Taylor said from close behind her. He nudged her forward. Ria, entranced, inched toward the manger. Above it, angry red fists were flailing. The swaddling clothes had been kicked aside. Ria looked down at the naked girl child.

Taylor cleared his throat and apologized for that one, small discrepancy. "I shopped around, of course, but the selection was limited. They were fresh out of boys." He slipped his hands beneath the infant, placing one under her buttocks and the other behind her head, and lifted her out of the cardboard manger. "But I sorta liked this one best anyway. She's got dominant Native American genes. See those cheekbones, that straight black hair? She reminded me of you. And she was kinda lonesome, having no parents who claimed her.

"As mayor, I pulled some strings with the county authorities. They consented to let us give her a trial run. They even consented to deliver her here and honored my unusual request that the nurse slip out the back door when she saw us coming. If we decide we like her, we can go down to the courthouse tomorrow and fill out all the necessary documents."

Ria's face was wet with tears of joy. "You mean she's . . . she's . . ."

"Ours." He handed the baby to her. "Merry Christmas, my love."

THE EDITOR'S CORNER

February is a favorite LOVESWEPT month. After all, it's the month dedicated to love and romance—and that's what we're all about! Romance is (and should be!) more important in our lives than just one special day, so LOVESWEPT is claiming February as a whole month dedicated to love. What a wonderful world it would be if we could convince everyone!

In this special month, we have six marvelous books with very pretty covers. In our LOVESWEPT Valentine month we have given all of our books covers in pink/red/purple shades—from pale pink confection, to hot fuschia pink, to red-hot-red, and passionate purple. This is our way of celebrating the month—so be sure to look for the SHADES OF LOVESWEPT covers, and we know you'll enjoy all the stories inside.

Our first book for the month, **STIFF COMPETITION**, LOVESWEPT #234, by Doris Parmett, is a heart-warming and very funny story about next door neighbors who are determined not to fall in love! Both Stacy and Kipp have been burned before and they go to ridiculous lengths to maintain their single status! But he can't resist the adorable vixen next door and she can't stop thinking of the devil-may-care hero of her dreams. When Kipp finally takes her in his arms, their resistance is swept away by sizzling passion and feel-

(continued)

ings telling them both that it's safe to trust again.

TOO HOT TO HANDLE, LOVESWEPT #235—This title tells all! Sandra Chastain's new book is full of sexy flirting, outrageous propositions, and hot pursuit. Matt Holland is a man after Callie Carmichael's classic convertible—or is it her cuddly, freckled body? Callie's not interested in any city slickers like Matt because she's a country girl living a free and easy life. But his kisses are too wonderful and they are bound to change her mind . . . and her lifestyle!

Next we have **SHARING SECRETS,** LOVESWEPT #236, by Barbara Boswell. We first met Rad Ramsey and Erin Brady in an earlier Barbara Boswell book, **PLAYING HARD TO GET,** which was a story about their siblings. Now Barbara has decided that Rad and Erin deserve a book of their own—and we agree! Sexy heartbreaker Rad knew women found him irresistible, but he'd always enjoyed the chase too much to keep the ladies whose hearts he captured. Erin had never known the fiery thrill of seduction, but Rad's touch awakened a woman who would be satisfied with nothing less. When they found each other, Rad knew he couldn't ignore his feelings and Erin knew she wanted this powerful, sensual, and loving man. This is a provocative story of a woman's first real passion and a man's true love.

Those incredible men surrounding Josh Logan are just fascinating, aren't they? Kay Hooper gives us another of the wonderful romances in what Carolyn Nichols calls the "Hagan Strikes Again Series" next month with **UNMASKING KELSEY,** LOVESWEPT #237. There is a terrible aura of fear hanging over the sleepy little town of Pinnacle, and beautiful Elizabeth Conner figures prominently in an episode that brings Kelsey there on the run and brings danger to a boil. Elizabeth also figures prominently in Kelsey's every thought, every dream . . . and she finds him utterly irresistible. This is one of Kay's most gripping and sensual romances and it seems to have "Don't You Dare Miss Me!" stamped all over it!

There's no more appealing Valentine story than
(continued)

MIDSUMMER SORCERY by Joan Elliott Pickart, Loveswept #238, an unforgettable story of first love—renewed. Fletcher McGill was back in town after six years and Nancy Forest was still furious at the man who captured her heart and then deserted her. They've been lonely difficult years and now Nancy is determined that Fletcher feel the full force of her hot anger—but instead, desire still flamed in her. Fletcher's touch scorched her, branded her with the heat that time and distance had never cooled. This time was his love as real and lasting as his passion?

We end the month with **THE PRINCE AND THE PATRIOT**, LOVESWEPT #239, a terrific book from Kathleen Creighton, a favorite LOVESWEPT author. This Valentine features a prince, some crown jewels, a European dynasty and a wonderful happy-ever-after ending. Our heroine, Willa Caris, is not a princess but a patriot. She's committed to protect the crown jewels of Brasovia, the small European country that was her parents' birthplace. Nicholas Francia is a prince in hiding and Willa doesn't know the truth behind his playboy facade. Carried away by tempestuous desire, Nicholas and Willa surrender to their intense attraction and need for one another . . . believing that the goals in their "real" lives are at odds. When the surprising truth is revealed, their love for each other proves to be as strong as their love for their traditions.

Remember to look for the six Valentine covers and spend the month in love—with LOVESWEPT!

Sincerely,

Kate Hartson

Kate Hartson
Editor
LOVESWEPT
Bantam Books, Inc.
666 Fifth Avenue
New York, NY 10103

The first Delaney trilogy

Heirs to a great dynasty, the Delaney brothers were united by blood, united by devotion to their rugged land . . . and known far and wide as

THE SHAMROCK TRINITY

Bantam's bestselling LOVESWEPT romance line built its reputation on quality and innovation. Now, a remarkable and unique event in romance publishing comes from the same source: THE SHAMROCK TRINITY, three daringly original novels written by three of the most successful women's romance writers today. Kay Hooper, Iris Johansen, and Fayrene Preston have created a trio of books that are dynamite love stories bursting with strong, fascinating male and female characters, deeply sensual love scenes, the humor for which LOVESWEPT is famous, and a deliciously fresh approach to romance writing.

THE SHAMROCK TRINITY—Burke, York, and Rafe: Powerful men . . . rakes and charmers . . . they needed only love to make their lives complete.

☐ RAFE, THE MAVERICK by Kay Hooper

Rafe Delaney was a heartbreaker whose ebony eyes held laughing devils and whose lilting voice could charm any lady—or any horse—until a stallion named Diablo left him in the dust. It took Maggie O'Riley to work her magic on the impossible horse . . . and on his bold owner. Maggie's grace and strength made Rafe yearn to share the raw beauty of his land with her, to teach her the exquisite pleasure of yielding to the heat inside her. Maggie was stirred by Rafe's passion, but would his reputation and her ambition keep their kindred spirits apart?   (21846 • $2.75)

LOVESWEPT

☐ *YORK, THE RENEGADE by Iris Johansen*

Some men were made to fight dragons, Sierra Smith thought when she first met York Delaney. The rebel brother had roamed the world for years before calling the rough mining town of Hell's Bluff home. Now, the spirited young woman who'd penetrated this renegade's paradise had awakened a savage and tender possessiveness in York: something he never expected to find in himself. Sierra had known loneliness and isolation too—enough to realize that York's restlessness had only to do with finding a place to belong. Could she convince him that love was such a place, that the refuge he'd always sought was in her arms?

(21847 • \$2.75)

☐ *BURKE, THE KINGPIN by Fayrene Preston*

Cara Winston appeared as a fantasy, racing on horseback to catch the day's last light—her silver hair glistening, her dress the color of the Arizona sunset . . . and Burke Delaney wanted her. She was on his horse, on his land: she would have to belong to him too. But Cara was quicksilver, impossible to hold, a wild creature whose scent was midnight flowers and sweet grass. Burke had always taken what he wanted, by willing it or fighting for it; Cara cherished her freedom and refused to believe his love would last. Could he make her see he'd captured her to have and hold forever?

(21848 • \$2.75)